THE FLOWER SHOW
THE TOTH FAMILY

THE FLOWER SHOW
THE TOTH FAMILY

István Örkény

*Translated by Michael Henry Heim and Clara Gyorgyey;
introduction by Michael Henry Heim*

A NEW DIRECTIONS BOOK

This English-language edition of *Rózsakiállitás* (*The Flower Show*) and
Tóték (*The Toth Family*) is published by arrangement with ARTISJUS,
Agency for Literature, Theatre and Music of the Hungarian Bureau for
Copyright Protection, Budapest.

Manufactured in the United States of America
First published clothbound and as New Directions Paperbook 536 in 1982
Published simultaneously in Canada by George J. McLeod, Ltd., Toronto

Library of Congress Cataloging in Publication Data

Örkény, István, 1912–1979.
  The flower show.
  (A New Directions Book)
  Translation of: Rózsakiállitás; Tóték.
  I. Örkény, István. Tóték. English. 1982.   B D B
II. Title.   III. Title: The Toth family.
PH3291.O35A24   894'.51133   81-22373
ISBN 0–8112–0836–2   AACR2
ISBN 0–8112–0837–0 (pbk.)

New Directions Books are published for James Laughlin
by New Directions Publishing Corporation,
80 Eighth Avenue, New York 10011

A European with a Hungarian Passport

Toward the end of his life István Orkény (1912–1979) enjoyed the satisfaction of seeing all his books sell out in a matter of days and all his plays fill theaters to capacity. In each of the Eastern-bloc countries a small group of writers enjoys a similar satisfaction. They are writers who have had to wait for more liberal regimes to see their works in print, and their extraordinary popularity stems from their integrity as well as their talent, since in countries where literature is a component of public policy, integrity is maintained at considerable cost: years in labor camps or prison, years of humiliation, years of silence.

Of course, the point of departure differs from country to country and individual to individual. In the case of Orkény, who might be called a European with a Hungarian passport, it lies squarely in the humanist tradition. Like Chekhov, Orkény was more interested in identifying and formulating pertinent problems than in proposing solutions. Solutions invariably enlist the latest ideology, and any ideology, with its patent on the truth, tends to emphasize the end at the expense of the means. Perhaps that is why, again like Chekhov, Orkény preferred compact genres like the novella and the play. And perhaps because both genres provide an evening's entertainment with roughly the same amount of material, he chose to dramatize several of his own novellas. Two of the resulting plays, *The Toth Family* and *Catsplay,* have had successful runs throughout Europe and America and been made into equally successful films.

Orkény was also a consummate practitioner of the short

story. He even devised a miniature genre all his own, the "one-minute fiction," and published several collections—short collections, needless to say—illustrating its virtuosity. Ranging from several lines to several pages, the tales encompass whole lives, whole epochs, but in the last analysis their goal remains modest: to pinpoint the absurdities of modern life we have come to accept as normal.

If we examine Orkény's work as a whole, however, we find a more ambitious goal. His ultimate concerns are universal; they include morality, loyalty, alienation. But even these are secondary to his concern for freedom. Orkény is obsessed with freedom. "How much freedom does a man have?" he asks in ways that vary skillfully from work to work. How is he to hold onto it? How can he make the best use of it?

Given recent Central European history, Orkény had ample opportunity to ponder the issue. No sooner had he begun to earn a name for himself as a writer than the war broke out. First he was drafted into the army; later he did time in a Soviet POW camp. Between his repatriation and the imposition of Stalinist norms on Hungarian literature he managed to publish a few volumes dealing with his war experiences. Then he fell silent for a number of years. By the time *The Toth Family* appeared, in 1964, he had regained enough freedom to write about freedom, and his outlook is typically Central European.

Fifty years earlier that quintessential Central European, Kafka, jotted a casual one-line entry in his diary about the declaration of another war, the war that became World War I. By treating it so blithely—it is all but lost in his description of a day spent pleasurably by the river—he was indirectly expressing the helplessness that he, a member of a small nation, felt in the face of world history. Orkény felt it too. (Not surprisingly, he once said in an interview that he "learned from Kafka as a son learns from his father.") He was constitutionally incapable of seeing war in heroic terms, in the style of, say, contemporary Soviet literature. For Orkény, war was the ultimate grotesquerie.

In *The Toth Family* he shows war at one remove in the person of a half-crazed major on sick leave. The Toths welcome him and even kowtow to him in the hope of helping their son, who is supposedly serving under him at the front. Unbeknownst to them, however, their son is dead. They are demeaning themselves for nothing. The major is a perfect illustration of Hannah Arendt's theory of the banality of evil, and the Toths are perfect targets for his inane brand of oppression. They rush to pledge devotion when submission would suffice. Toth is one of the most common Hungarian names, and Orkény is doubtless making a reference, none too veiled, to his compatriots' double capitulation: to fascism during the war and Stalinism after it. Like the Hungarians, the Toths revolt in the end, and the why and how of their revolt supplies the novella with a satisfying finish.

While acknowledging a debt to Western literature of the absurd, Orkény never entirely identified with it. Indeed, he differed fundamentally from the absurdists in that he believed in a way out. He did not claim to know the way out—the denouement in *The Toth Family* is as grotesque as the incidents leading up to it and has no validity as a practical solution— but he so structures his works as to give the impression that somewhere, somehow it exists. For all the absurdity of the characters and their antics, Orkény places them in history, in concrete situations that move forward instead of coming full circle.

If *The Toth Family* demonstrates Orkény's penchant for the grotesque, *The Flower Show,* first published in 1977, shows him equally at home in the realist tradition. Although the scene and characters are those of Budapest, the idea behind them came to Orkény in New York. Switching on the television set on the last day of a visit to America, he happened to see a documentary on death and dying. It set him thinking. How would an analogous program look in Hungary? And what if instead of merely interviewing the mortally ill the up-and-coming young documentarist contracted to film his subjects while they died and catch the actual moment of death, the transition between life and death?

Orkény chooses the subjects carefully: a professor of linguistics, a woman who works packing flowers, and a popular

TV news commentator. Each represents a different segment of society, a different frame of reference, a different set of prejudices. The role of the news commentator is particularly telling because in him Orkény makes most explicit the issue he raises in one way or another on every page: how the very fact of reporting the news influences the news, that is, how it alters what actually happens. By severely limiting the number of factors involved, he throws the issue into sharper focus than many of the recent non-fiction articles and books that have tried to account for it.

But he does more. By implication he is also examining the relationship between art (represented here by the contemporary "genre" of the television program) and life (represented here by death). The irony implicit in both does not detract from the resolutely humanist conclusion: that art can and does influence life and, consequently, that the artist must answer for what he creates. By no means did Orkény wish to place strictures on the artist's freedom; he suffered too much from them himself. He was simply reiterating in modern terms the age-old message that freedom without responsibility or, at the very least, freedom without accountability is tantamount to tyranny.

Michael Henry Heim

THE FLOWER SHOW

Translated by Michael Henry Heim

Death is not one of life's experiences; death cannot be lived.

Wittgenstein

Death is the only muse.

Dezso Kosztolanyi

The Minister of Culture
Budapest

Sir:

Please forgive me for turning to an important and highly placed official like you for something that will perhaps seem insignificant, but for three years now I have been active in television as an assistant director without receiving a single serious assignment. As soon as I suggest a topic, it is rejected. My documentary *How We Die* is a case in point: I have been refused permission to proceed with it. Death is an unsuitable topic because everyone is afraid of it, they say, but I say the reason people are so afraid is that we never talk about it and have no way of knowing what it is. Now that the number of believers has dropped and we have lost the consolation of the other world, all we can do is make stabs in the dark at something dreadful, something fearful against which we have no defense.

Why this silence? It does no good, it only makes matters worse. Things used to be different, and not only because people could have faith in the resurrection. No, there was something else: most people died at home surrounded by relatives and friends. Nowadays the act of death nearly always takes place within hospital walls, and more often than not we spend our last hours in the company of a doctor or nurse who is an utter stranger to us. Objectively, from the point of view of the care of the patient, this may be more beneficial, but subjectively, from the point of view of a man facing death, it is much more frightening. Paradoxically enough, it has taken modern society to turn death into a mythical concept: death—an organic part of life, its

3

necessary end, the driving force behind all human work, creative activity, and progress.

What I mean to do is break into this vicious circle by showing the television audience the last hours of three terminal patients. I have already found three people free enough from prejudice to volunteer for the film, but I must stress that although they have volunteered, their services are not gratis. All three wish to leave whatever they receive to their survivors.

This complicates matters. According to the present regulations the station is authorized to pay out royalties to trained actors only, and dying is not in the same category as acting. I must therefore request your financial support as well.

I believe in the significance of my film. Television is the first medium in the history of the arts to provide us with the possibility of introducing a mass audience to patients suffering from incurable diseases, to give that audience the priceless gift of the patients' most dramatic moments. It is my desire to be as tactful as possible and avoid all shock effects. I do not wish to offend the viewers' sensibilities or their taste.

My immediate superiors—and their superiors as well—have refused me permission to proceed with the film on both material and ideological grounds. But I am confident that an important, highly placed public official such as yourself, a man with your broader perspective, will recognize the moral significance and educational impact a film of this sort could have. If I have succeeded in convincing you of the importance of my venture, kindly do whatever is in your power to make it a reality.

In the hope of a positive response I remain

Yours respectfully,
Aron Korom
Assistant Director

♦   ♦   ♦

Aron received no response at all. He began to mope. He would treat anyone in the station buffet to a cherry brandy for a chance to give vent to his frustration, but he found no sympathy. Suicide, pure and simple, everyone told him. That's not the kind of material documentaries are made of, not here at least.

4

Soon he had made enemies of almost everyone and had to do his drinking by himself. One day, when by eleven in the morning he was on his fourth brandy, Ularik sat down at his table.

"Drinking, I see," he said. "Then I guess there's no point in waiting around."

"Waiting around for what?"

"You sound like a rank beginner. You know what I mean. Where's my treatment, my camera, my cameraman, my studio requisition, my crew?"

"What crew?" Aron was dumbfounded.

"For the documentary *How We Die.*"

"The one you banned?"

"We don't ban anything here. It's just the title I don't like. But there's plenty of time to argue about that."*

"You mean you'll get it approved?"

"I already have. Everything's set. Ready to go. Can't you even say thank you?"

"Thank you."

"Now who's going to do your camera work?"

"I don't care. Give me a chance to think, will you?"

"We'll find you someone who won't talk back. As good as deaf and dumb. How many days will it take to shoot?"

"No idea."

"What do you mean? We have to take long-range planning into account, you know. Budgets and studio schedules."

"Well, I can't very well order my subjects to die according to plan, can I?"

"But I have to tell the bosses something."

"That's what you always say. Can't you make them see that the program is about them, too. One day even they will run out of breath. Aren't they interested in what will happen then?"

"All I want is some idea of how long it will take. A month? Two months? A year?"

"I don't know. As soon as my last subject dies."

* Ularik, who was head of Documentaries, won the argument. Instead of *How We Die,* which sounded too serious, the film was televised as *The Flower Show.*

5

"That's a new one on me, but I guess you young fry can get away with anything. When can you start?"

"As soon as I have what I need."

"Write up your treatment and you'll have it all tomorrow."

"Then I start tomorrow."

♦ ♦ ♦

"Is this the Darvas residence?"

"Yes, it is."

"May I speak to Gabor Darvas?"

"Who is this?"

"Aron Korom. From the TV station."

"Oh, it's you. Unfortunately my husband died last week. The funeral was Tuesday."

"I'm very sorry to hear it."

"Where did you disappear to? Poor Gabor and I talked a lot about you."

"It's taken me all this time to get permission to go ahead with the program."

"Too bad. But tell me, do you still want to hear about my husband? Because if so, I'll be only too glad to stand in for him."

"What do you mean?"

"Let me be frank with you. That small sum you're offering would come in very handy right now. So if you're still interested in Gabor's death, I can go to the studio and tell the story of his last ten days straight into the camera. It would be better if Gabor were still alive, of course. I just hope you don't think I'm trying to break into television."

"Not in the least. When will you be able to make it?"

"Any time at all. After work, that is."

"Then I'll be waiting for you at the station tomorrow night at seven."

♦ ♦ ♦

He was given a small studio on the side of the building facing a playground. The soundproofing was so bad that the sounds of children laughing and playing came right through the wall. But that's all right, thought Aron. It won't hurt to break up the gloomy mood with a little background gaiety.

Mrs. Darvas was in mourning. They sat her against a light-colored curtain without any scenery or props. Aron asked her to talk directly into the lens and said that if she got tired or was overcome by emotion she could take a break.

"I won't let my emotions run away with me. I won't take a break."

She sat down. Aron glanced over at the tight-lipped cameraman as a sign that everything was ready to roll.

"How We Die. Mrs. Gabor Darvas. Part One. Take One."

◆ ◆ ◆

My husband died ten days ago after seventeen years of a not particularly happy marriage. I will use his name, even though you've offered me complete anonymity, because he was so well known in his field that anyone the least acquainted with it would recognize him anyway. His name was Gabor Darvas. We went to the university together. I became a teacher—Hungarian and French; he did research in Finno-Ugric linguistics. In other words, he became a scholar. We were in our third year when we got married. For a long time we had to make do with a room in someone else's apartment. It took eight years for us to get our own—an efficiency with all the conveniences, but cramped. Oh, we could have gotten along fine if we'd had a little more in common, but I—with my outgoing, expansive character, my desire for a full social life—was hardly compatible with Gabor, the dignified workhorse whose reserve slowly degenerated into total silence. In the morning he would drink his coffee without a word, already deep in the day's work. Then he'd go to the university, and after lunch in the cafeteria, he'd work in the library. For dinner he'd have some yogurt and a piece of bread and butter and then sit down at his desk. Looking back on it all now, I've come up with an explanation for his breakneck schedule. Perhaps he had a premonition his time was short. Perhaps the reason he pushed himself so hard was that he wanted to be able to follow up his first book—which was a great scholarly success—with another. He didn't quite manage it. A long time ago he began complaining of a pain in the back of his neck, but he refused to take time out to see a doctor. This is no place to go into what was wrong with him, but finally he spent two weeks in the hospital in very bad condition. When at his own request he was allowed to come home, the pain subsided a bit. He stopped having dizzy spells so often and began to perk up and feel better. "Is he over it?" I asked the doctor. There was a long silence. "He's the only one who thinks so," he answered. "You must be strong now, Mrs. Darvas. We've done everything in our power, but the time for the operation that might have done some good is long past. All he has is a few weeks left. I can't even promise you a month."

I took him home in a taxi. We stopped off at the university library for him to take out a few books, and as soon as we got home he set to work. For years we had said almost nothing to one another. If we talked at all, it was only when absolutely necessary. But that evening when I took his yogurt in to him, he suddenly said, "There's something I want to ask you about. You had a talk with the doctor, didn't you? I don't care about my health. All I need is three good months. Please, inform me what he said."

"Please inform me," "Let me inform you"—that was the way he always spoke. I had no idea what to say. What could I tell him? To forget those three good months? Maybe I should have concocted some fairy tale. I couldn't make up my mind. To gain time I lied. I told him they had asked me to go back to the hospital the next day and talk over the results of the tests with the doctor.

"Then you will inform me tomorrow what I may expect."

I had one more day.

I gave it a lot of thought. I weighed all the arguments and then went in and told him the truth: "You'll have to use your time well, Gabor. You have only a few weeks left."

I realize my decision requires an explanation. My husband never lost his temper, never became emotional. The only time he showed any feelings at all was during our romance at the university, and that died down quickly enough. Before long I ceased to exist for him. All he cared for was his work: the application of structuralist techniques to the study of Finno-Ugric languages. I didn't understand it, ergo I didn't exist. I could look beautiful or a mess, I could be healthy or sick, I could have friends over, make noise, turn the radio or phonograph on full blast—he never even looked up. Strictly speaking, *he* didn't exist either. His organism was merely a device for completing a certain amount of work a day. He had no desire; he never longed for the sea; he never felt any Christmas spirit. Telling him he had only a few weeks to live would be more or less tantamount to telling him there was a paper shortage and he wouldn't have enough to finish his book. That's what was going through my mind that evening—and half the night. Meanwhile, he worked till dawn.

The next day after lunch I took a chair over to his desk. I had to say his name twice before he reacted. I had a lot of trouble getting through my prepared statement. He didn't blink an eye. In fact, he went right back to his manuscript. But since I didn't leave while he leafed through it, he finally had to take notice of me.

Now please don't misunderstand me. I'm not complaining. If he didn't show me the first book when he brought home his author's copies (it has since been translated into three languages), well, that was all right. I wouldn't have understood a word of it anyway. And I can't really say I was unhappy with him. He never yelled at me, he never hit me. Indifference causes no pain—just a void, a feeling of failure. It may sound strange, but it was my cruel death message that won me the first victory in fifteen years.

"Thank you for being so candid," he said calmly, almost warmly. "Now perhaps I can salvage whatever is salvable. Tell me, can you type fast enough for me to dictate to you?"

"I think so."

"What a wonderful woman you are, Anna."

9

I couldn't believe it. He remembered my name. I asked him what I could do to help.

Together we restructured the last section of the book, taking into account the three week deadline. To make the most of my services, he had to initiate me into the mysteries of his field. Fortunately I have a good head, and it wasn't long before I mastered all I needed to know. Suddenly it dawned on me: for the first time in fifteen years of marriage I had achieved equality. I started as a typist, moved on to girl Friday, and ended up a full-fledged colleague. Every day we worked three shifts: morning, afternoon, and evening. Three weeks equals twenty-one days, which made sixty-three work periods in all.

"Only, of course, if all goes well and my brain holds up."

That was the only thing he feared. Not death.

"Why argue with death?" he once remarked. "All death can say is no."

By then he had begun talking to me during our breaks. About nature, for example. Nature may have created a great masterpiece in man, but she didn't learn a thing from it. She was still just like she'd always been: helpless, apathetic, a silly fool. The only way to treat her is with audacity: stand up to her, milk her for all she's worth.

Which is just what he did. He called the hospital to find out whether or not they could use his kidneys for a transplant. The hospital agreed to take them. At about the same time a young television director came to see us. He was making a film about death and wanted to know if Gabor would mind being one of his subjects. Not only did he not mind, he was very pleased with the idea. He made two conditions though: that he not be bombarded with questions and that his schedule not be interrupted by the technicalities of making the film. The director agreed to respect them. Unfortunately for all of us, he came back a week too late. The reason I am here now is to make good my husband's intention and tell the story of his last ten days for him. Ten days is all he got of the three weeks we'd planned for. Not quite half.

The disease that attacked Gabor in the prime of life can

take one of two courses: either, as the doctor predicted in Gabor's case, there is a gradual deterioration, an erosion of consciousness stretching over a period of weeks, even months, or an abrupt, violent end—what the doctors call the "rapid" variety. Suddenly something snaps, and it's all over. This sudden form of deterioration set in on the tenth day after Gabor returned from the hospital. He died on the evening of the fourteenth day. First his left leg was paralyzed, then his right. Next it spread to the entire lower half of his body. The doctor came and examined him and then sat down on the edge of the bed. Naturally I had told him on the phone that my husband knew everything.

"Is there no way out?" Gabor asked the doctor.

"At times like these we usually say that miracles can happen."

"Well, I don't believe in miracles. All I really need is another week of work."

"When there's no way out, we all feel the need for one more week. Shall I have you sent to the hospital?"

"No."

"Then I'll be back tomorrow morning."

We worked all night. The best we could do with the last chapter—a summary of the arguments followed by a conclusion—was to outline it briefly. We never even got to the thirty or so typed pages of material meant for footnotes. At dawn we slept a few hours, but soon I was back at the typewriter again. Even though Gabor's right arm was paralyzed by then, his brain worked on without a hitch. I had to call the hospital to tell his regular doctor not to come. Every minute counted. The only person I let in was the local doctor, and all he did was give Gabor a shot of painkiller. Then back to work.

"What do you think?" asked Gabor. "If you put down the section headings and I dictated the basic ideas paragraph by paragraph, could you write the last chapter?"

"You can't be serious."

He admitted it was just a pipe dream and asked me for a cup of coffee. While I was making it, he suddenly began to scream. It was the first time in my life I ever heard him raise his voice, curse, use profanity. Out of respect for him I won't repeat any of it.

It was a dreadful sight. Normally when a person swears, he throws his body around and gesticulates violently. But even Gabor's left arm was paralyzed by then, so the curses spewed forth from an absolutely motionless body. Why it was I don't know—that's the reason I'm bringing it up—but instead of cursing his illness or the doctors or death, he cursed Aron Korom, the television director, who hadn't been back for weeks.

"That worm! That dirty rotten liar!" he screamed. "What kind of fool does he think I am?"

Who invited him? Why did he come? Why did he say Gabor's death was a matter of public concern? That it had a moral for everyone? That its message was eternal? Was he just trying to make himself seem important or did he have some scheme in mind? That's the way those film people are. Why isn't he here now with his camera? How else is the world going to see what a worm man is? How else will they see how we kick the bucket before we're half way there, before our work is done. And why? Because we forget to take into account we're three-quarters animal. We've discovered fire, conquered the seas, put an end to the plague; we write panegyrics to our kind. But what about him? Take a look at him, Gabor Darvas. He can't pick up a pen much less finish his life's work. People will never even know he was paralyzed. They'll go on living the life they've always lived—a long line of animals, unseeing, unconscious, unsuspecting.

I stood there holding the coffee as though I were the one who was paralyzed. My husband had always been soft-spoken, self-contained. What could I do with this maniac? I tried to pull myself together. Then I yelled at him as if there were a wall between us, "Quiet now, Gabor dear. It's time for your coffee."

In a split second he was calm again. It was like magic. Maybe it had to do with my forceful tone of voice or the

12

"Gabor dear" he hadn't heard since our university days. He wasn't the type for pet names. Diminutives are scarcely in keeping with absolute invincibility.

I sat down next to him, lifted his head, and gave him the coffee sip by sip. By then he wouldn't even have been able to hold the cup in front of his mouth. He asked for a cigarette. I had to hold the cigarette for him, too. When he'd finished, he said in his old, impassive voice, "Too bad the television director didn't see that."

"What?"

"That cigarette."

"Would it have made things easier for you?"

"Somewhat," he said. "It would have done my paralysis some good as well. And that last smoke would have been preserved—on videotape at least." I am reproducing his words as carefully as I can.

Now that he'd gotten the rage out of his system, he felt like working again. "Bring the typewriter over, darling, and don't answer the door." It was the first time he had called me "darling" in years.

I was able to complete eighteen more pages, the first third of the last chapter. He stopped short in the middle of a sentence. When I looked up, he was no longer breathing. By the time I got over to him, his heart had stopped beating. He hadn't suffered at all. His hands lay open on the comforter; his head had sunk deep into the pillow. The second half of that sentence he took away with him into the void.

Well, that's what I wanted to say now that he can't say it. It wouldn't be right for me to speak about myself, but there is perhaps one thing directly connected with his death I might mention. When I go back over our seventeen years of marriage, I have the feeling I was never really his wife until those last ten days. Maybe it puts me in a bad light, but the only time I was happy with him was when he was dying.

◆ ◆ ◆

13

Dear Mrs. Miko,

It took the station a long time to receive permission to film the program, which is why I am writing you much later than I promised. Perhaps you do not even remember my speaking to you in the hospital about a matter which you not only had the moral fortitude to understand, but in which you also heroically agreed to assist me. I would be very disappointed if you have since regretted your decision, as I have now completed the first part of the program, an account of the last days of a scholar by his widow. Both the woman involved and I were very satisfied with the results. I will do everything in my power to ensure that your involvement in the venture will proceed in a manner befitting the gravity of the occasion.

Yesterday I had a talk with Dr. Tiszai, who told me as much about your condition as medical discretion allows. Among other things I learned that two weeks ago you were released—driven home in an ambulance—to care for your mother until something more satisfactory can be worked out. As a result we will have to do our filming in the apartment—with your consent, of course. We promise to inconvenience you and your mother as little as possible. Now I have another big favor to ask of you. If the viewers are to have any real appreciation of your case, they must know a little about its background. What I have in mind is a re-enactment of the morning when, after taking stock of the situation (including the situation at home), Dr. Tiszai disclosed the nature of your illness to you and told you what to expect.

Without seeing all this, the audience will not be able to make sense of what follows. Dr. Tiszai, who is a great patron of the arts, has agreed to cooperate. I have left it with him that if you give your consent, an ambulance will come and take you back to your old hospital room for an hour. As soon as the filming is over, it will bring you home again.

I realize I sound as though I am going back on my word: I promised that there would be no play-acting, that you would not be required to do anything theatrical. But if we fail to recreate your talk with the doctor, the audience will have no way of understanding what your illness involves, how it will develop, and where your mother and her problem fit in. Granted, we never discussed anything like this, and it will not be easy. But I hope that so considerate and understanding a woman as you will

14

agree to my request. The reason I am writing to you beforehand is to give you time to think it all through. I hope you will give your consent.

In conclusion, I am glad to be able to inform you that I have succeeded in obtaining a contract from the station for the same amount we agreed on orally (five thousand forints on the first day of shooting, ten thousand when you die—to be paid to your mother). On Wednesday, when I come to see you in person for your decision, I will bring the contract with me so we can both sign it.

In the hope you are still willing to cooperate, I remain,

Aron Korom

◆ ◆ ◆

Neophyte directors have a good many surprises in store for them. Aron had not yet seen his best laid plans come to grief in front of the camera. He did not know that all expectation is delusion, that nothing is absolutely certain.

Take the scene in the hospital room, for example. Who would have thought that an uneducated, unskilled laborer like Mrs. Miko would be so calm, so articulate, that she would speak neither too fast nor too slow and show not the slightest trace of stagefright. Or that the doctor—a great reader, art collector, and theater-goer—would be so unnerved by the camera that he would fidget continually and break down in the middle of every other sentence. They began three times and gave up three times.

"How about a cup of coffee?" Aron suggested.

"No thanks," said the doctor. "Let's get it over with."

"Ready?" Aron asked the cameraman.

"Ready."

The doctor screwed up his courage. He turned to the sick woman lying on the bed, took her hand, and gave it a little pat. His voice was still trembling, but that only made his words sound more lifelike.

"You work in gardening, is that right, Mrs. Miko?"

"Oh, not anymore. Six weeks ago when I got sick, they

15

transferred me from gardening to packing. Now I tie the flowers together."

"And where is it you work?"

"At the Tisza Nursery in Budafok. We do more than just weddings and funerals. We do a lot of exporting, too."

"And is your new work less strenuous?"

"The work itself, yes. But I have to work the night shift a lot—getting two or three thousand roses ready for the late flights. The next day at noon they're on sale in Vienna or Stockholm."

"Your husband lives abroad, doesn't he?"

"Yes, somewhere in America. I haven't heard a word from him in twenty years."

"Do you have any children?"

"No, none."

"But you support your mother, who—if I remember correctly—has glaucoma."

"That's right. All she can see now is blurry outlines of things. She's completely dependent on me. . . . Tell me, when can I go back to work?"

"That's just what I'm here to talk over with you. May I call you Mariska?"

"Go right ahead. But why? Is there something wrong?"

"Don't be frightened, Mariska."

"I'm not frightened. It's just that Mama won't be able to get along without me. During the day when I'm at work, it's all she can do to heat up the soup."

"I'm sorry," said the doctor getting up from the bed. "I can't seem to remember what happened next."

"You recited some poetry," prompted Mrs. Miko.

"Oh, that's right. Damn it. Now I'm going to have to start all over again."

But Aron assured him he could go on from there and recite the poem: he'd have to edit the film in any case. The doctor sat back down again.

"I know a poet who also happens to be a doctor. Ida Urr is her name. This is one of her poems:

16

Night falls, they put her to bed,
She looks up and hopes
The colorful reeds of her hope
Will embellish the night
At least one more night.

"Very nice," said Mrs. Miko.

"The reason I recited it, Mariska, is that I don't want to deprive you of hope. But I don't want to give you any false hopes either, if only because of your mother and her future. And we'll have to take care of her one way or another: unfortunately, you have cancer."

"Cancer?" asked Mrs. Miko. "Isn't there any cure for cancer?"

"For many kinds, yes. But in your case there's nothing we can do. Be brave. We can give you a sedative if you like."

"No, I'm all right."

"Well then, try to get a little sleep."

"Not now. I have to start thinking over what this is going to mean to us."

"I respect your strength of character, Mariska. Other people in your position go completely to pieces, and once they start weeping and wailing, it's almost impossible to raise their spirits again."

"Well, as far as I'm concerned, death is a matter of money. What will become of my mother when I'm gone? That's my main problem now."

"Is there anything I can do?"

"You can tell me whether or not I can go back to work. If I have to stay in bed for a long time and get put on sick pay, we'll never clear our expenses."

By now the doctor had been infected by Mrs. Miko's calm behavior. He had stopped fidgeting and looked straight into the camera. He had even forgotten he was acting. He concentrated entirely on his patient, calmly explaining that she would no longer be able to work because what she needed most now was a good rest. She could go on doing the housework for her

17

mother though, and there would be plenty of time to find the right home for her.

"I can't put her in a home. She's almost blind."

"Then maybe she can go to a home for the blind."

"No, that's no good either. She *can* see, after all, and she'd never allow anybody to treat her like she was blind."

"It's awfully good of you—and brave too—to think about others instead of yourself," said the doctor. Then he remembered this was how their talk had ended, so he stood up.

But Mrs. Miko reached out for his hand and sat him down again. She wanted to ask him whether he wouldn't let her work even one month more because this year was the first country-wide flower arrangement contest and the Tisza Nursery had very good roses. So the extra month wasn't for the money. She had been entered in the contest, her project had been approved. And after all the torture she'd gone through with those roses, was she going to be deprived of the glory of the award ceremony?

"You've got to resign yourself to the fact that you're not capable of working anymore, Mariska."

"I realize that."

"And that you won't be seeing your roses again."

"If that's the way it has to be."

"But don't be afraid. Don't despair. It won't hurt, I promise."

"Only Mama will hurt, Dr. Tiszai."

"Stop! That's it for today," Aron called out. "Thank you."

He congratulated the doctor and Mrs. Miko both for having played their difficult parts so naturally that there would be no way of telling it was actually a reconstruction.

Mrs. Miko smiled proudly. Just as the television crew finished packing, the ambulance men came in for her.

♦   ♦   ♦

The first sign of trouble was that Mama could not stand Aron, mostly because she thought he had offered them too little for what she called "our performance." She had decided that a better established, more famous director would have paid them much more. If only she had been in charge. That daughter of hers was completely hopeless. It never even occurred to her to try to boost the price.

Mama had been even more put out when the crew began setting up for the first session in the apartment.

It did not take long for anyone to see that the cameraman was going to have a hard time of it. Mrs. Miko and her mother lived in a dark tenement building. Their apartment had been turned into two units twenty-five years before and had remained exactly as it was all those twenty-five years. The window of the smaller room opened onto a balcony that ran all the way around the courtyard and was therefore in constant use. The larger room was quite long, but as narrow as a hallway. It was cut in two by the double bed Mrs. Miko slept in. The largest room was the kitchen. Part of it was originally meant to be a bathroom, but all that had ever materialized was the showerhead protruding from the wall.

They had no choice. The only thing they could do was rearrange the furniture in the long narrow room. They moved the bed over to the window and the wardrobe into the kitchen. Then they hung their lights from the ceiling. The comings and goings were bad enough, but—much worse—the new set-up made it impossible for Mama to find her way around the apartment.

Not only that. She soon realized she would constantly be in the way. Since she almost never went outside anymore, she spent all her time lolling around the apartment. Moreover, her only joy, her last passion, was food. She had put on so much weight that if she sat on the bed with her daughter, she blocked her completely, filling the whole screen. They finally took care of the problem by pushing two kitchen stools up against the wall for her. Oddly enough, the incident that triggered her pent-up rage was a remark Aron had made to get on the right side of her. "Make believe we don't even exist," he said. "Don't pay a bit of attention to us."

That was a terrible blunder. Oil on the flames. Perhaps if he had demanded something of her—a service rendered for a fee—he would have won her over. As it was, she exploded. What did he mean "not pay a bit of attention to them" when they'd turned the whole place upside down with their chiseling and plastering and hammering! And if that wasn't enough, he had the whole house going crazy. Everybody knew about the TV program being filmed at the Mikos'. Until he came the neighbors always liked them. Whenever they had a free minute, they'd lend a hand. But now—now they're all bursting with jealousy.

And in fact the entire building was in a frenzy. The balcony was constantly crowded with neighbors carrying on heated discussions about everything that happened inside. That first day, even before Mama had finished her tirade, the gypsy woman who lived upstairs came flying into the room demanding a part in the program: when Mariska was on night duty, she was the one who undressed the old woman and put her to bed.

Aron had no objections. He pointed the camera in her direction and said, "Go ahead, please. Go ahead. Say anything you like."

The straggly-haired woman flushed with excitement. Her whole body tightened up. She looked over at the director, pressed her hand to her heart, and cried, "Long live the fatherland!" Then, immediately calm again, she left.

The cameraman locked the door after her, but the mood was broken. Mama was quiet. Mrs. Miko was quiet. The crew had stopped working and retired silently to a corner. All that afternoon and the following day things remained the same. Sometimes for the sake of appearances Aron would start the camera running. If nothing else, it would get them used to it. And it did. By the third day Mama, who could hardly see the men anyway, had pretty much forgotten their presence and began a conversation that was more important than they were.

"Do you ever think about the future, Mariska?"

"It's all I think about all day."

"Do you think about who's going to get the apartment if you die?"

"You'll keep it, Mama."

"And what if they kick me out, if somebody with pull takes a liking to this gem of a place?"

"This is your official residence. They can't kick you out."

"Who says they can't? The only reason you say 'There won't be any problem' about everything is because it gets you off the hook."

"I've asked about it."

"Who? Your TV friends?"

"No. The day they took me back to the hospital I called old man Franyo. They let me use the phone. I told him how things were and asked his advice. The apartment is yours to dispose of as you see fit."

"Where does a gardener pick up that kind of information?"

"Old man Franyo knows everything. He says all I have to do is talk to the administration at the nursery and they'll help you."

"A lot of help they've been so far. Why do you think they transferred you to packing?"

"Because I was so weak."

"And they'd have less pension to pay."

"I asked about that too. Your pension will be based on my salary for the past three years, not only the six months I worked in packing. They're figuring out now how much you're going to get, Mama. They'll let us know. That's something we ought to be clear about."

"When will they let us know?"

At that very moment there was a ring at the door. Coincidence is sometimes a better director than the best of professionals. The cameraman opened the door, and in came four guests, right on cue: old man Franyo (one of Mrs. Miko's superiors at the nursery) and a family of three—Sandor Nuofer, his wife, and his son. They stood there in the doorway—obviously embarrassed by the presence of both the sick Mrs. Miko and the camera—until Aron ushered them in. They put down their packages and began introducing themselves and working their way through the mandatory small talk, to which Aron finally put an end by asking them to sit down and take part in the program as friends of the family. After a bit of hesitation they agreed to stay. "But first give us time to unpack what we've brought," said Mrs. Nuofer.

They did their unpacking in the kitchen. The nursery's employees had sent Mrs. Miko two fried chickens, a fancy custard dessert, a home-cured ham, cookies, a linzer torte, and an enormous number of eggs. The young woman laid the chicken out on plates and passed it around. Each of them took the little taste expected of them.

Then came the hard part: fitting all the newcomers into the already tight space. For a while they had no luck, but Mrs. Miko finally saved the day. "I'm still allowed to walk around," she said. "If we fold the bed up, we can put at least four people on it."

They helped her on with her housecoat, folded up the bed, and sat down. After making certain everything was quiet, old man Franyo began to speak. "I think some introductions are in order. My name is Franyo, and this is the Nuofer family. They're from the nursery as well. We are here because we have learned of the great honor Hungarian television has bestowed upon our Mariska. She herself has told us of her talk with the doctor, and we are deeply distressed. Everyone commiserates with you both. The women have done all this cooking and baking to save you work in the kitchen."

Mrs. Miko thanked him.

"The next time we come, we'll bring you more. In addition, the administration has authorized me to pass on to you eight hundred and eighty forints in aid."

He laid the money on the table. Mama counted it up and said sarcastically, "Well, now we don't have a care in the world."

"Quiet, Mama," said Mrs. Miko. "Thank you again."

"And how much will my pension be? Tell me that, why don't you?"

"We've just finished figuring it out. It comes to eighteen hundred a year. After Mariska's death."

There was a short silence, during which everyone did a bit

of mental arithmetic. Mama wanted to say something, but Mrs. Miko cut her off. "I *had* counted on more," she said softly.

"There's nothing we can do, Mariska. That's how much it comes to. We realize it's not enough for a sick woman to live on, especially one in need of outside help. Do you have any savings?"

"Only what the TV people are giving me."

"And how much is that?"

"We've already gotten five thousand so far, and Mama will get another ten thousand after my death."

"Which will just about cover the funeral," put in Mama.

"Isn't it too early to talk about funerals? . . . We suspected you didn't have much money, so we got together with the administration, and—well, that's why the Nuofers are here. You know them, Mariska, don't you?"

"Of course."

"And you know what good people they are. The boy is quiet. Sandor doesn't drink, doesn't smoke. Both he and his wife work, and they have twenty-two thousand forints in the bank."

"And they want to give it all to us?"

"Quiet, Mama."

"You'll see what I'm driving at. Tell them why you're here, Sandor."

"My wife will do a better job than me. She finished school." Mrs. Nuofer took the floor. "We live in a basement apartment. When it rains, the water seeps in through the plaster. In the summer the air is extremely humid and as a result very harmful to our boy. When we went to Franyo here with our troubles, he told us we were in luck: it so happened, he said, that before long this kind old woman would be left alone in a three-room apartment, which is just what we need. In exchange, we will give her the contents of our savings account and sign a contract to support her for life and look after her. I promise we'll be good to her and give her everything she needs."

Mama took a long look at the Nuofers and asked, "Your husband's not a gypsy, is he?"

"He has a dark complexion, but he's not a gypsy."

"I just wanted to make sure he doesn't slip my pension into his pocket on the sly."

"Your pension is no business of ours."

"Except that you'll let me pay rent and electricity and gas out of it."

"Only a quarter of each. We'll pay the rest."

"And where does food fit into your little plans?"

"If you see fit, you can contribute a small amount. If not, that's all right, too. If there's enough for three, there's enough for four."

"It's easy to sound big-hearted now, but how do I know you won't change your tune when you're the one in command?"

"Just ask your daughter," interjected old man Franyo. "She'll tell you how trustworthy they are."

"My daughter doesn't understand a thing about this kind of business," said Mama dismissing him with a wave of her hand. She looked the Nuofers up and down. "What do you cook in— fat or oil?"

"Oil, but if you like, I'll use fat for you."

"That's what I am accustomed to. I should also tell you I have a sweet tooth."

"I baked the linzer torte we brought. Here, try it. Please."

Mama took a bite and chewed it slowly, carefully. Then she took another. And another. She closed her eyes as if she were trying to catch the strains of some beautiful, distant music. Finally she nodded.

"Edible. But that doesn't bind us to anything. For one thing, I can't stand the racket children make."

"Oh, he's very quiet," said Mrs. Nuofer.

"That's his problem—he's too quiet," added her husband.

Mama still wasn't satisfied.

"I don't like quiet children either. Now tell me. If we don't get along, can I break the contract?"

"Yes, you can," said old man Franyo trying to reassure her, "if they don't fulfill their obligation to support you satisfactorily."

"And when do they want to move in?"

"Right away, while the weather's good," said Mrs. Nuofer. "We don't want our son to get TB."

"Well, *we* don't want to be rushed, but we don't have any choice in the matter," said Mrs. Miko standing up with both her hands pressed to her stomach. "Bring the deposit book and write up the contract, and move in while the weather's good. But now please go home. I'm tired, and I'd like to lie dwon."

"Right there is where it should end," said Ularik after seeing the first rushes. "Death mitigated by social solidarity. I know what they want upstairs. It's just right."

"But it's not enough," said Aron.

"What are you after anyway?"

"I haven't the faintest idea. I can't even try to guess where this thing is going to lead me. The way I left it with Mrs. Miko—if anything happens, she'll let me know."

"What does 'anything' mean?"

" 'Anything' means anything. If a miracle happens and she starts improving. Or if not and she starts getting worse. Anything is possible. That's what makes life interesting. You can never tell what's in store for you."

"Don't be crazy. Look, you've got a good educational film on your hands. Why take chances?"

"But it's not anywhere near finished. I still have one subject who hasn't been in front of the camera yet."

"Who's that?"

"J. Nagy."

"The writer? You must be kidding. He's in great shape."

"But he's had one heart attack already."

"Six years ago. And if I know J. Nagy, he'll breathe his last in the arms of some hot blonde."

"He'll have another heart attack. You wait and see."

"But when?"

"I don't know, but I can wait. And then get it on film."

"If he lets you."

"I've asked him, he's agreed. And J. Nagy is a man of his word."

"That's true."

"Then there's nothing to worry about."

Aron had exaggerated a bit, but only to the extent that the promise had been made in the garden of an out of the way drinking establishment in Buda under rather less than sober circumstances. Aron had begun his television career as J. Nagy's assistant on a documentary series. Despite the great difference in their ages they became friends, perhaps because they were both men of great vision.

J. Nagy had been to the front as a journalist and later wrote a book about his experiences there (*Notes of a War Correspondent*). He went on to publish a collection of stories and a novel, both of which disappeared from the literary scene without a trace. Finally he took a job in radio, and soon he was a top newsman. Television, as far as he was concerned, was invented especially for him. He completely abandoned literature and began grinding out TV scripts, very few of which ever reached the screen. Gradually he came to the realization that he had more ideas than imagination and needed to be on good, firm ground if he was ever going to go anywhere. So he switched back to documentary and news work. By the time he was ready to make his breakthrough, he had been unofficially categorized as class B material. To make matters worse, he had begun putting on weight. They implored him to go on a diet, but eating and drinking meant so much to him he could not lose an ounce. Finally he turned out a series that proved viable: a dozen in-depth interviews with famous actors. Then, encouraged by his success, he made a follow-up called *Great Men of Science,* which popularized him, the witty moderator, much more than science or the scientists. Since *Great Men,* however, he had done nothing at all.

He and Aron had discovered a small place in Buda where all they served was good dry sausage and wine. They went there often to drink and talk things over. Together they would pull apart Ularik, who foiled their best synopses, and weave bigger and better projects.

"Some day I'd like to make my own documentary," said Aron once in a fit of wishful thinking.

"What about?"

"About how people die."

"With actors or real people?"

"It wouldn't be interesting unless they were real."

"Go to, Aron my boy! It's a terrific idea."

"It's more than an idea, J. Nagy. Look at all it covers: science, philosophy, poetry. And besides it's fascinating, the kind of thing everyone can relate to."

"But can you find a subject willing to die in front of millions of eyes?"

"How about you?"

"Oh, I've got a long way to go yet," said J. Nagy with a laugh.

"You've had one heart attack already."

"All right then," said J. Nagy with the largesse that comes of having had a drop too much. "My next heart attack is yours."

"That's very kind of you."

Such was the promise. Made in a questionable garden restaurant after an unknown quantity of spritzers when the program existed only in the realm of Aron's imagination.

The first place to look for J. Nagy was the station buffet. He was always surrounded by beautiful women: they enjoyed being fondled by a famous writer and laughed uproariously at his wise-cracks. If a punchline had the desired result, he would lean back in his chair, a satisfied smile turning up the corners of his mouth.

Aron called him out into the entrance hall and reminded him of his promise.

"Do you really need me?" asked J. Nagy.

"I really need you."

"Give me till this evening to think it over."

♦　♦　♦

They met at their usual table.

"First listen to my objections," J. Nagy began.

"Remember how you said your project would combine poetry, science, and philosophy? Well, that's a lot of hot air, my friend. In the first place, because death is ugly and slapdash and art is all beauty and composition. And in the second place, there's no philosophy in a one-time thing like death. Philosophy is all generalizations. So philosophy's out too. And with science you're even farther off course. Any physicist will tell you that during the observation of minute and sensitive processes the mere presence of instruments of observation distorts the course of events. In other words, the death I die in the presence of the camera will differ from the death I would die if, say, only Aranka were present. So the scientific value of your film is nil, no more than an illusion."

"What you mean is you're backing out."

"All I'm trying to do is tone down your ambitions. Forget about art and science. Shoot it as you see it. Make an honest documentary. Go about it as if you wanted to show a group of divers working underwater on a bridge. The only unusual thing is that in your film the divers drown."

"You've got something there."

"If you take my advice, you can create something absolutely unique."

"Something you would take part in?"

"Why not—if its time has come. I'm interested in everything new. Besides, I haven't done a thing for a year and a half. Ularik has been trying to involve me in a documentary on air pollution, but I'd rather die than do that. An aging exhibitionist like me will go to great lengths for a juicy role. . . ."

"I knew you'd do it."

"Now, since you're my director, tell me what you want me to do."

"Nothing yet. Have you been seeing a doctor?"

"What for? I feel great."

"For your heart."

"No complaints in that department either."

"That's immaterial. From now on I want you to have a cardiogram done every week. Let me know as soon as the slightest change shows up."

"You have a long wait ahead of you."

"I hope so."

"Well, good luck."

"You too."

◆　◆　◆

A week went by. Aron had a free evening and felt like a few drinks. On the spur of the moment he went down to the buffet to find J. Nagy. He found Aranka Tocsik, his divorced wife, instead.

"Waiting for J. Nagy?" asked Aron.

Who else? The in-crowd knew they were getting married again. (If they actually went ahead with it, it would make J. Nagy's fifth marriage.)

"I've been sitting here an hour and a half," said Aranka.

"The way we left it, he was just going to run over to the clinic for a second. What have you done to J. Nagy anyway?"

Everybody called J. Nagy J. Nagy—both his divorced wife and his short-term women. The latter came and went, but always came back. By his own account they would pant "Bite me, J. Nagy, bite me!" into his ear when they made love.

"It was only friendly concern that made me ask him to have those cardiograms done."

"Well, you've set off an avalanche. What are you pushing him into anyway?"

"I'm not pushing him into anything. All I wanted was to have a few drinks with him."

He left quickly to avoid the rest of her lamentations. It was also common knowledge that J. Nagy kept postponing the wedding because of a young actress. To marry Aranka, he had to break with Iren (the actress's name was Iren Pfaff). First Aranka would tip the scales in her favor, then Iren in hers. As far as J. Nagy was concerned, however, women were completely interchangeable. There were times when he called Iren "Aranka" and times when he called Aranka "Iren." He lived only for his art.

Stepping into the elevator on his way from the buffet, Aron

Korom found himself standing next to Iren Pfaff. The actress did not return his hello.

"What have I done, Iren?"

"I feel like having you drawn and quartered."

"Because of my friend, you mean?"

"If he really is your friend," she said getting off the elevator, "stop torturing him like this."

That evening Aron decided to drop by their haunt just in case. Sure enough, there was J. Nagy sitting in the arbor with a pitcher of wine, a bottle of soda water, and a thick book spread out over the smooth wood table.

"What's that you're reading, J. Nagy?"

"Magyar and Petranyi's *Internal Medicine*."

"What in the world for?"

"It doesn't hurt to keep an eye on those doctors."

Then he explained why.

The first doctor he went to see was one Aranka Tocsik recommended. After doing the cardiogram, the doctor told him he had nothing to worry about as long as he took it easy. Wait a second, said J. Nagy to himself. If I have nothing to worry about, why do I have to take it easy? The next day, for safety's sake he paid a visit to Iren Pfaff's doctor. My findings show nothing wrong, said doctor number two, so you're free to go walking and swimming and give your heart a good workout. Well, which was it going to be: should he take it easy or give his heart a workout? So J. Nagy went to a third doctor and a fourth. Each of them reassured him, but each of them reassured him in his own way. J. Nagy was thoroughly confused. He went from one doctor to the next in search of a precise and definitive diagnosis. Finally he found it in the hospital of internal medicine attached to the University. Dr. Szilvia Freund, his doctor there, was a pretty woman with a somewhat military bearing. She recognized him at first sight. She had seen the actor interviews and the *Great Scientists* series and treated him with the respect due their originator. After a thorough examination she informed him of the results. "You've had one heart attack already. If you want to prevent another one, stop smoking, avoid unnecessary excitement, and stay away from heavy foods."

"But I'm not sick, am I?" he asked nervously.

"No, you're not sick. But you're not well either."

Seeing his frightened face, Dr. Freund tried to calm down her famous patient by picking up the cardiogram and giving him a minute explanation of each squiggle. J. Nagy took out a pad and noted it all down. By the time she was done, he had a pretty good grasp of the rudiments of the field. He asked if he could take the cardiogram with him and was on his way out the door when Dr. Freund called him back. "Sit down please, Mr. Nagy. I want to take your blood pressure again."

"Just call me J. Nagy," said J. Nagy.

"Gladly. But I must tell you, my dear J. Nagy, that even if we take your age into account, your blood pressure is higher than it should be."

"What is taking my age into account supposed to mean?" He was insulted. "I have no age."

"*You* look young for your age; your blood pressure unfortunately, doesn't. Don't get too upset though. We'll bring it down for you."

She wrote out some prescriptions, which J. Nagy brought into the station together with the cardiogram. At first people did not take him seriously when he waved them under their noses: hadn't he always bragged about his indestructible constitution? They assumed he was joking, and they laughed.

Only Aranka did not laugh. Just to be on the safe side, she wanted to have a talk with the new doctor. The next day they stopped in at the hospital together.

"I've brought along my former wife. She's very worried about my blood pressure."

The two women looked each other over from tip to toe. After taking J. Nagy's blood pressure again, Dr. Freund said, "High, but not dangerously so. Avoid all forms of excitement. And don't expect any improvement from one day to the next."

But the next day J. Nagy was back, this time accompanied

by Iren Pfaff. Now *these* two women scrutinized one another carefully.

"Actually it reads a shade higher than yesterday," said the doctor after taking J. Nagy's blood pressure. "Are you sure you haven't been under some kind of strain?"

"Definitely not," said Iren. "Maybe it's not accurate."

With a condescending smile Dr. Freund picked up the apparatus and went into a detailed explanation of the principles behind it and their practical application. J. Nagy was so inspired he went straight to a medical supply store and bought one.

He even tried it out right on the spot with Iren assisting. She turned out to be very good at it.

"If I were your wife, I could take your blood pressure every day. You wouldn't need to go to the hospital."

"Let me think it over, darling."

He thought it over, then sat down at the typewriter and typed out the identical letter, word for word, to both Aranka and Iren.

For as long as my blood pressure is high, I had better avoid the excitement of getting married. As for having it (my blood pressure) taken, I'll muddle through on my own somehow.

Love and kisses,
J. Nagy

And with a bit of trial and error he actually did figure out how to take his blood pressure by himself, all by himself. After filling in Aron Korom on these recent developments—and consuming quite a bit of wine and soda water—he gave a demonstration. "See? It's still high," he said pointing at the gauge, "even though I've stopped smoking, eating rich food, drinking coffee, and seeing Iren and Aranka. Their constant talk of marriage was a major source of stress."

"I don't believe it," said the director with a laugh. "You've turned into a hypochondriac, J. Nagy."

"Is this the kind of gratitude I get? From you of all people! You who know what I'm preparing for."

"With a fat-free diet? What *are* you preparing for?"

"My role."

"Nobody's asking you for a medical degree."

"If I'm going to have any concept of what the role entails, I have to know what's in store for me."

"Watch out you don't scare yourself out of your wits."

"And you watch out you don't let your feelings run away with you. We're professionals, not dilettantes. An artist can show no mercy."

"Has your blood pressure gone down at all?"

"Unfortunately not."

"Really? Then it's time to put you in front of the camera."

"What do I say?"

"Whatever comes to mind."

"Will anyone care?"

"Your audience will, J. Nagy. The more alert and vibrant you look now, the more impact your death will have."

"But you don't want to make it seem like I'm condemned to death, do you? You wouldn't use a cheap, tasteless gimmick like that."

"But think how powerful it will be. I've got a studio reserved for tomorrow."

"I won't have anything worth saying about death until I start dying."

"Just wait till you see the final product. You'll be great, I promise you."

"Yes, but I won't ever have a chance to see the final product."

"Oh, I guess you're right."

◆　◆　◆

I don't suppose I need to introduce myself to you, the television audience: you've seen me many times before on your screens. Perhaps you remember the interviews I did with some of our fine actors or the *Great Men of Science* series. I come before you now in a different capacity: instead of encouraging others to unburden themselves, I will unburden myself. This short talk is a prelude to a very important event for me. When the time comes, I am going to die before your very eyes. Six years ago, when stricken with a heart attack, I made a journey to the other shore. It was a journey from which I barely returned. Moreover, during the war I served as a correspondent at the front and witnessed one of history's worst examples of mass carnage. I can safely say I've seen all the variations death has to offer.

But it is not only my personal experiences that have prepared me for this role: as soon as I accepted it, I began familiarizing myself with the scholarly literature on the subject. As a result I can state without compunction that I am ready for my final appearance.

I realize that most of you have never seen so much as a tooth being pulled on television and that you may well run and switch off your sets in horror if you see me weeping, wailing, and flailing about. But please don't be afraid. I promise to remain cool and collected, to avoid the slightest tinge of naturalism, and—insofar as the subject matter allows—to leave pleasant feelings. I hope to see you all again at my deathbed.

Thank you.

♦　♦　♦

For two weeks nothing happened, or rather, the only thing that happened was that the Nuofers borrowed the nursery's truck and moved in with Mrs. Miko and her mother.

Aron and his crew turned out in full force for the event, but instead of going up to the apartment they did all their shooting outside. The truck pulls up. Out come the beds. The bedding goes up in baskets. A lamp is left standing on the sidewalk in the way of passersby. That was all they needed: it was only filler.

A few days later they drove out to the nursery. They happened to choose a good time. Everything was in bloom, and there was a lot of activity going on: it was almost time for the flower show. They got some good long shots of the rose beds. This, too, Aron wanted only as filler, background material. He was not at all sure he would find any use for it.*

Then came a long period of waiting. Finally a letter arrived from Mrs. Miko. "I am very weak now," she wrote in a shaky hand, "and I want to talk to you alone. You can come in mid-morning when the Nuofers are gone. We'll have to find some way to get rid of Mama, too."

It turned out to be easier than they had expected.

Mama opened the door. "Who's there?" she asked. "Not the TV people, I hope."

"Sorry, it is."

"What do you want this time?"

"We've brought some chocolate, and we'd like to have a word with your daughter."

"I guess you can come in then. And when you're done with her, I have something to say to you too. Only I don't want her to know about it."

"Then you wait in the kitchen, all right?"

◆ ◆ ◆

They had brought Mrs. Miko a salami, sliced ham, and some mixed salad. "I can't see myself *ever* eating anything like that again," she said. She was much thinner, much weaker. She seemed lost in the large double bed. Only her stomach was large. She asked them to prop up her back with pillows.

"Is it all right to go ahead?"

"We're ready."

"It's Mama I want to talk about."

"Could you tell us something about yourself first? How do you feel?"

"Worse and worse. Unfortunately, it wasn't true what he said about it not hurting. At night I take sleeping pills, so all I do is moan in my sleep, but during the day my stomach stretches so tight I'm afraid it's going to rip open. They give

---

* He did. The field of flowers provided an excellent, highly effective contrast to the scenes of Mrs. Miko dying.

me plenty to eat, but I don't dare touch it. Every bit I take—I'm afraid it's going to burst. But I didn't mean to complain about my stomach. There's nothing I can do to change that. No, what's really bothering me is that I'm not at peace with myself and can't talk to anybody about it. Not even Franyo. He'd be terribly hurt. He was only trying to help when he suggested the Nuofers move in. It's not his fault I'm more worried about my mother than before they came. That's why I wrote you the letter."

"Let's talk about Mama."

"I'm getting to it. I realize that what I'm saying now will one day be on television, so I want to make it clear they're good people. The way they've divided it up, Sandor takes care of Mama, his wife looks after me. Unfortunately I'm more work every day. First because I can't get up to go to the bathroom and have to use a bedpan, but also because there are times when I have to throw up, and if it comes on me unexpectedly I have to be cleaned up afterwards. And that means an extra load of wash, too, because I don't have a lot of sheets and pillowcases. We've been poor all our lives, but we've always put cleanliness first. They're the same way. Look, see how the floor shines. That's Mrs. Nuofer's work, and she does it mostly late at night. I don't think there's a hospital in this city where I'd get the kind of care she gives me. But that's not what I asked you here for. What was I talking about before?"

"Mama. You wanted to talk about Mama."

"Oh, yes, of course. It's been eight years now since she started having trouble with her eyes, and as her sight got worse, she got more and more demanding. She's like a little child. Give her a finger and she wants a hand. And ever since the Nuofers moved in, she's been absolutely impossible. Back when I still had the strength for it, I would take her out shopping with me. Now she has Sandor Nuofer take her out for a walk every day. In the evening she plants herself in front of the television, but since she can only hear the sound, she keeps pestering Sandor to tell what's going on the screen. He'll do anything for her—anything she comes up with. Every day around noon—twelve noon!—she starts asking me to look at the clock. 'Why isn't Sandor home yet? I hope nothing's happened to him.' You'd think I'd be happy for Mama and feel better about her future, but the more she worships Sandor, the more of a burden I am to her. Oh, if I'm thirsty, she'll get me a cup of tea, and she brings in our meals—Mrs. Nuofer is a good cook, and Mama's appetite is gigantic—but she never bothers to see if I eat anything or take my medicine, and she absolutely refuses to touch the bedpan. Her excuse is she's afraid of bumping into something with it. I really wish my end would come. The longer I drag on, the harder I make it on the Nuofers, and that only hurts Mama's prospects. I don't know. Have I made myself clear? Do you see why I'm so worried about the future?"

"Tell us more if you like. We've got time."

"The doctor comes every day to examine me, but he's stopped saying anything except what a good patient I am and how little I complain. I realize what that means, and the rest of the day I worry over what's going to happen here once I'm gone and the Nuofers are legally entitled to share the apartment with Mama. True, they'll still be obliged to support her, but how long will they keep it up? They're tired when they come home from work. They can't go on waiting on her hand and foot like this much longer. Then Mama can play up to Sandor all she wants. He won't tell her what's going on the screen; he won't take her out for walks. Her free ride will be over. They'll forget she ever existed. And why? The Nuofers' first allegiance doesn't belong to Mama, it belongs to their son, and Mama can't stand the sight of him. Things are quiet now, but there's a storm in the air, and when it breaks, there'll be hell to pay. The reason I asked you to come is that one day when I'm gone, you'll show this on television, and they'll all be sitting here watching—the whole family. Can you tell me which way to turn so I can look Mama straight in the eye?"

"Just look straight at the cameraman."

"I'm looking at *you* now, Mama. You know how difficult you are. I want you to try to live in peace with the Nuofers. Don't be hard to please or demanding. And most important, be nice to the boy. Talk to him. Make sure he does his homework. Make believe he's your grandson. You can't see well anymore, and you need people to help you. Eat what they eat. Thank them when they do something for you. Do it for me, Mariska, your daughter. It will bring me peace when I'm lying in my grave. . . . Thank you, boys. You can take the pillows out from behind my back now."

Mama was waiting for them in the kitchen, lost in her own thoughts, staring out into nothing with empty eyes. The weak light filtering in from the courtyard ricocheted from one corner to the other. There was a hundred watt bulb hanging from the ceiling, but they decided not to turn it on.*

"You can go ahead now."

"Just take a look around. Do I have to say a word? Things haven't been this bad since the war. Here in this kitchen is where we get washed, where we cook, where we do our laundry, and where the Nuofers' jittery little brat sleeps. When he slept in the small room, he saw shadows moving past the windows, so they made up a bed for him on the cold stone floor, and how am I supposed to see him down there with my bad eyes? So I've tripped over him twice. And they had the nerve to go and complain to my daughter! Can't I even move around in my own apartment? And who do you think is the cause of it all? Let me tell you right to your faces: you are! Who are you doing all this for I'd like to know? What good is it? Why should anybody care what happens to us? We got along all right till now without anybody knowing we existed. Then you turn up with your TV cameras, and everybody goes crazy. They stop doing what they feel like doing and start lying and carrying on because they're scared stiff of making fools of themselves in public. How many times do you think old man Franyo dropped by before you came along? He came here for one reason and one reason only: to show the people at home watching TV how good the Tisza Nursery is to its workers. And as soon as the Nuofers got wind of his tricks, you can be sure they didn't waste a minute. That woman—she makes believe she can't live without staying up all night emptying bed-

---

* The idea proved effective. By shooting the scene in semi-darkness, they showed the old woman's world the way she herself saw it.

pans and washing puke off sheets. And Sandor—now there's a real gypsy for you—lying all the time. I'm the only one he enjoys watching television with, he tells me. And then he takes me out for walks and tells me what he sees on the street. Well, two can play that game as well as one. I can lie too. I'd do anything for my poor daughter's sake. So we fall into each other's arms and make a great fuss over each other, but at the same time each of us knows what's going on in the other's mind. How do I stand it? Well, I don't really mind it. I can see they need a place to call their own, but I hope we haven't gotten to the point where an apartment like this can end up in the hands of a gypsy. It's a little run-down at the moment, of course, but give it a fresh coat of paint, plane down the floor, tile the bathroom and put in a tub and a sink, and this place could bring in a mint. You don't think so? Well, you will when I tell you—now don't go blabbing this to anybody—I've had a much more attractive offer than that contract old man Franyo foisted on me. A lawyer—a woman—has offered me exactly twice as much for the apartment as the Nuofers' savings account, and along with the money she's going to do a complete renovation job. She's been here twice now—in secret, of course: I don't want poor Mariska to get wind of this. She's a good cook, too. You'd have to go a long way to find a jelly roll like hers. And most important, she has no kids. Just the two of us. It would be like having another daughter."

"But you've signed a contract, haven't you?"

"The lawyer lady's had a look at it. As an interested party she doesn't want to interfere, but the contract that can't be broken has yet to be written, she says."

"So you'd throw the Nuofers out onto the street?"

"Oh, I'd give them back their bank book."

"That wouldn't be very nice of you, would it now?"

"Don't tell me *you're* going to give me a lecture. You of all people. The cause of it all. Why didn't you just let my daughter die in peace? She may be good with her hands; she may work hard and know a thing or two about roses, but when it comes to money she's absolutely lost. I'm the one who took care of her salary for her. Every time she went out shopping, she'd ask me what to buy and where to buy it. Then you come along with your fifteen thousand forints and old man Franyo throws in the gypsy's bank book—of course she's going to lose her head. You can't blame her for wanting to show what good care she's going to take of her old mother. Even after she dies. And why not give her the satisfaction of thinking she's been a good daughter? But the minute they've shoveled the earth over her coffin, I'm taking over. And then this apartment goes to the highest bidder. It's about time, too."

"You don't mean you want your daughter to die, do you?"

"All I want is for her to have peace and quiet as long as she lives. What happens afterwards is my affair. Just don't go blabbing any of this to anybody."

"Don't worry. We won't. But everything you've just said will be part of the program."

"When will you show it? Before the funeral?"

"No, well after it."

"Well, I won't have any secrets then."

"Thank you for your candid remarks," said Aron.

He looked back at the cameraman without saying a word and turned on the light. The hundred watt bulb cast a sudden harsh light on her.

♦ ♦ ♦

On the way back to the studio they sent Sandor Nuofer a telegram in care of the nursery in Budafok, asking him to come and see them at the station the next day after work.

He came, but refused to set foot in front of the camera. Why didn't they ask his wife? She had an education, she wouldn't be nervous before a big audience. But during the conversation it became clear that the family was in dire need of money: the apartment they'd moved from had been furnished, so they still had to lay out money for furniture, and even though what they brought was old and broken down, they were still twenty-five hundred forints in debt.

When Aron offered him the twenty-five hundred, he decided to go ahead with it. The only trouble was, he didn't have any-

40

thing prepared. And he was in his work clothes. Don't worry they said soothingly. That's even better.

♦　♦　♦

"Please tell our viewers, Sandor Nuofer, whether you find taking care of Mrs. Miko a burden."

"Well, it keeps us busy, but that's what we expected when we signed the contract. And to tell the truth, we never dreamed she'd be such a good patient. We help her, but she helps us too."

"She helps you?"

"My son, well, he never did very well in school, and we don't have much time to spend with him. But now, as soon as he comes home, Mariska goes over the day's lessons with him. Even when she's in pain. His grades have shot way up. You see, I don't care that much about the work I do. All that matters to me in life is my son. I don't know what's going to happen when Mariska goes. I can't get up the courage to talk it over with my wife."

"But you can tell us. Is Mama the problem?"

"Yes, she is. But the audience isn't interested in *her.*"

"Why don't you tell us how you've been getting along with her?"

"At first everything was fine. We tried to overlook her bad points. She *is* half blind after all. And besides, it was important for us all to live in harmony. Well, it worked for a while. Then the troubles began."

"The troubles?"

"I'd be ashamed to talk about them here."

"But we're really interested, Mr. Nuofer."

"Well, it all started at meals. All she likes is rich, heavy dishes and dessert. Goulash and jelly rolls—that's all she'll eat. But you can understand, can't you, Mr. Korom, that with Mrs. Miko to take care of, my wife can't cook two different meals every night. We're happy when Mariska can keep down a few spoonfuls of cream of wheat or chicken broth or custard, and of course we eat what she eats. But the old woman—she sits down at the table, cuts herself a big piece of bread, smears

41

it with fat, pours on the salt, and with a great show of suffering chews away to her heart's content. Or else she'll have me bring some cans of, say, stuffed cabbage into her room and then sit there and wolf down two or three portions—cold, straight from the can. Not a pretty sight, but we didn't even let that get to us."

"And what *did* finally get to you?"

"I can't help it: I see everything from the point of view of how it affects my boy, and I can see quite plainly from the way she treats her own daughter, who's completely at her mercy, what will happen afterwards when she's shut up there with my boy. It's not very promising—that's for sure."

"Does Mama neglect her daughter?"

"When you're sick, you need a lot of attention. We leave early in the morning and don't come back till dinner time. Is it right for my wife to do everything? Mariska is in such a bad way she has to be bathed every day. Now that's something Mama could take care of. Even with her bad eyesight. But no, she won't touch her. She forgets to give her her pills and leaves the bedpan to stink under the bed all day. The only thing she does is warm up her lunch for her. She doesn't love her daughter. Believe me, she doesn't. I bet she'd try to speed things up if she could."

"Is she really that bad?"

"My wife—she finished school, and she puts it another way. She says it's revenge."

"Revenge?"

"She says she's taking revenge on everybody who can see. Look, she says, she's attacking her own daughter now. Why? Because she puts up the least resistance. And who's next? Our boy. She's kicked him twice already, you know."

"She told us it was an accident."

"Well, we know better. It's still light in the kitchen when our boy takes his afternoon nap. Even with cataracts she can tell he's there."

"Why not bring it up with her? It's in everyone's interest to clear the air."

"As long as Mariska's alive, I'm not opening my mouth. I

talk nicely to her, I watch TV with her, I take her out for walks—anything to keep up appearances. If you came and stayed with us, you'd think every day was a holiday. But it takes a superhuman effort on my part. Especially since my boy has begun behaving so strangely."

"Can you be specific?"

"He seems like a different child. He won't go out and play. We never hear him laugh. He jumps at everything; he's lost his appetite, and he can't get to sleep at night."

"You mean you blame all that on Mama?"

"My wife does. You see, our boy has always had weak nerves. Two years ago he tried to commit suicide after bringing home a bad report card. Fourteen years old! True, he only took ten aspirin and then threw them up right away, but even so we took him to the psychiatric clinic. They made us promise never to scold him. They said what he needed was praise, rewards, reasons for being happy. Since then, of course, we've done everything to make life easy for him, but who knows what will go on in that apartment once he's shut up there alone with Mama. So you see, we're in a very bad position. We can't live without that apartment, but our boy is more important to us than life itself."

"What would happen if one day you had to make a choice between the child and the apartment?"

"I've never given it any thought."

"Of course you have. That's all we've been talking about all this time."

"Well, I don't know. Believe me, Mr. Korom, I'm a quiet man, a peace-loving man. I never drink more than a bottle of beer, and I've never raised my hand against anybody. But when it comes to my son, well, that's something else again. When it comes to my son, I wouldn't stop at anything."

"What do you mean?"

"If anything happened to my son, I'd be capable of murder."

"But you just said you'd never raised a hand against anybody."

"But that would be the end of the world for me. I'd pick up the first heavy object I could find and beat her to death."

43

"I certainly hope there won't be any cause for that, Mr. Nuofer."

"So do I. Any more questions?"

"No."

"Well, then I'd better be going. The stores will be closing soon, and I want to stop off and buy a chocolate bar for her."

"For Mama?"

"When my child's well-being is at stake, I'm willing to try the impossible."

"Good luck, Mr. Nuofer."

♦ ♦ ♦

J. Nagy had suddenly disappeared. Iren Pfaff was the last to see him, and all she knew was that he had gone to the hospital for a three day check-up. She had driven him there in her car. She had been a bit surprised that besides his pajamas and slippers he took along nothing but medical books and journals. But what was even more surprising was that for two whole weeks he had not given a sign of life.

One day during the second week Iren came at visiting hours with a grilled chicken and a plate of potato salad, but Dr. Freund intercepted both chicken and salad and informed her that J. Nagy was not allowed to have guests.

Nothing can remain a secret very long at the station.

The next day Aranka Tocsik turned up at visiting hours with a large baking sheet of homemade apple strudel. But *she* got only as far as the afternoon nurse, who was happy to relieve her of the strudel, but refused to let her in to see J. Nagy.

This episode also made the rounds of the station. It was even embroidered on. By the time it reached Aron, J. Nagy had fallen ill because of his work on the program and would have to spend the rest of his days in the hospital. That was the last straw. In no time he was knocking at the door of Dr. Freund's office, armed with his tape recorder, three bottles of wine, and three bottles of soda water. She received him coldly.

"Why have you come? J. Nagy is not allowed guests."

"I just wanted to hear you say it."

44

"Sit down," said Szilvia. "Let me make some coffee, and we can have a little chat."

They sat there drinking coffee, trying to outguess one another. There was no love lost between them. Dr. Freund immediately took the offensive. She demanded that J. Nagy be released from his part in the documentary because the excitement surrounding it was undermining his health. Until he was roped into the project, he had never given death a second thought, which is quite unusual for his age group. Now he thinks of nothing else, and we are faced with a paradoxical situation: death has become his only goal in life. At least part of the reason why his blood pressure has shot up is psychosomatic. And although we've managed to bring it down to normal during the past few weeks, we have also found evidence of circulatory insufficiency. In technical terms, a minimal ST elevation is present in the third and fourth precordial leads, which as far as you're concerned, means that his cardiogram is starting to look bad. If we can't do anything about it, he'll be in for a heart attack—and soon. "Of course, he doesn't know a thing. I can count on your discretion, can't I?"

"Don't worry. All I want is to have a spritzer with him."

But Szilvia would not allow even that. Anything that might remind him of the documentary was harmful. All he had come in here for originally was a check-up, but he had yielded to her arguments and stayed on because he felt so safe within these walls. Besides, they protected him from his old circle of friends, who now seemed to him like so many reminders of his death. In self-defense he had decided to see none of them.

"Have you been able to make any progress with his cardiogram?"

"It takes time."

"Well, you can at least let him know I'm here."

"It won't do any good."

"And if you mention I've brought along three bottles of wine and three of soda water?"

"You don't really think he'd sell you his peace of mind for so little, do you?"

"I've known him longer than you have."

Dr. Freund left the room insulted. She was even more insulted when she came back with the message that J. Nagy would be happy to see him.

He was all by himself in a four-bed room surrounded by a rampart of books. He swept a few of them off a chair to make room for his guest.

"So you've brought your tape recorder along."

"Will it bother you if I turn it on?"

"Not at all. But first let's have some of that wine."

♦ ♦ ♦

Tape Number One*

"Let me begin by saying, Aron, that I haven't forgotten my promise."

"That's not the reason I'm here."

"I just wanted to get that straight. You know, the more I get into my part, the more I see where it's going."

"Well, I'm glad to hear it. For a while I thought you were trying to hide from me here."

"Just the opposite. I came here to get closer to you. What better place for our goals, for our work than a hospital? I feel so much at home here I don't think I ever want to leave."

"You mean you want to live in a hospital? That doesn't sound like the J. Nagy I used to know."

"Not live here, just take leave of life here."

"You've got plenty of time for that yet. I hear your blood pressure's down."

"Yes, they've brought it down, but my heart's not doing too well, thank God. Promise you won't tell a soul? Szilvia's forgotten that when I first came to see her, she showed me how to read cardiograms. Here, take a look. These are the last results. You see? It's absolutely plain: an ST elevation in the third and fourth precordial leads. In other words, first alarm. My best

* This dialogue, slightly cut, was used later on in the program as a voice-over for J. Nagy's funeral.

46

guess is that I have two or three weeks left. I'm just telling you so you can make the most of your time."

"But I'd be much happier if you got better, J. Nagy. They're spreading rumors around the station that I'm driving you to death."

"Lies. All lies. You can tell them from me that the main reason I decided to stay in the hospital is I can't stand the sight of them. Now that I've finally found something that's right for me, why go running back to that smelly station? Why stay what I was—a delivery boy taking his own talent from door to door. What choices would I have there? Either I'd marry Iren or remarry Aranka. And why start kowtowing to Ularik again? I've had enough. Tell them I'm on my way toward the light. My body is like a ragged slipper I've stepped out of. Now I can live for art. I have everything here I need: room, wine, soda water, and a doctor who—in case you haven't noticed— has the breasts of a Marilyn Monroe."

"Don't tell me *that* cold fish has gone and fallen for you."

"Let's put it this way. She doesn't deny me the tender attentions that ignite the creative mood."

"Don't you think you ought to forget your usual amorous intrigues? It's all I can do to get in to see you now."

"She'll soften up, Aron my boy. And if nothing else will do the trick, I'll marry her."

"You really do have everything you need here, don't you?"

"Maybe my theoretical background leaves nothing to be desired, but I do have some practical problems I can't take care of by myself. Will you give me a hand?"

"What do you need?"

"Take a look around. This hospital room is going to have to be our studio. It has a lot of open space, a lot of light—it seems fine. The thing is, downstairs on the main floor there's an intensive unit full of brand-new equipment for patients about to breathe their last. I've been down there to see it. It's really ideal. And we won't be able to use it."

"We won't?"

"No. We'll have to stay here. The only thing we can do is

turn this room into an improvised intensive care unit. All we need is a few pieces of that new equipment. Nothing more."

"Leave it to me. What else?"

"A telephone."

"Why not ask your doctor friend to get you one if she's so hot for you?"

"That's just it. She's a little jealous, and she's trying to keep me cut off from the outside world. Make a list of what I want you to do, all right? First, get my typewriter from Iren's apartment. And our telephone from Aranka's. Then take the typewriter out of the case and put the phone in instead and leave it downstairs with the man at the door. Nobody will look twice at a typewriter. Then if anything happens, I can let you know right away."

"You'll have your phone, but how am *I* going to get back in here? From what I've been able to gather, Marilyn Monroe isn't very happy about your role in the documentary."

"Call her in. Let me have a talk with her."

"How about a drink first?"

"Not a bad idea."

"Cheers."

"Cheers."

♦ ♦ ♦

Tape Number Two

"Would it bother you if I put this conversation on tape, Szilvia?"

"Not at all. I have no secrets. Now, what is it you want?"

"All we want is your approval. My friend, this young director here, is making a film about me."

"I know. But whether you like it or not, J. Nagy, I'm going to cure you, so the premise your film rests on is a bit premature."

"Sooner or later it will have to reach maturity."

"Well, that time is far off. And anyway a hospital is not a theater."

"This is no farce we're putting together; it's a serious documentary. Our goal is the same as yours: the advancement of science."

"That puts things in a different light, it's true. But still we're here to cure people, and what you're interested in, if I understand you correctly, is how people die. What made you choose a topic like that? I don't quite see the point."

"We chose it because we have no model for death, Szilvia. All we know is that it is out there waiting for us. We think of it as a leap into the darkness. Let's show the television audience that death is human. Let's call it by its name and give people a chance to picture it, grasp it."

"And where do I come in?"

"What we need now is a beautiful woman. Your beauty will enable the audience to swallow the bitter pill we're trying to feed them."

"Flattery will get you nowhere. I'm a doctor."

"But that's just what we need. You'll play the role of Dr. Szilvia Freund seeing her patient through thick and thin on his final journey."

"Let me say at the outset: I won't tolerate any meddling in professional matters."

"You have my word that you will be able to carry out your duties as usual. Now, do you accept?"

"I'll have to get permission from the head of my department."

"Then I'll have the station send him an official request for your services. Did you hear that, Aron?"

"Yes, I'll see to it."

"You're a wonderful woman, Szilvia. It will be a pleasure to work with you. Thank you, Aron. You can turn off the tape recorder now."

♦ ♦ ♦

Ularik's face lit up when he saw Aron come in.

"Finally! I hope you're here to tell me you're all done. Everybody's on pins and needles. You can't imagine the pressure I'm under."

"We're nowhere near finished."

Ularik's face fell. "One day you'll have to finish it, you know."

"Then give us some help."

"What sort of help?"

He must really have been under pressure because he promised to do all Aron's biddings: he would speak to Dr. Freund's superior at the hospital; he would ask permission to do the filming there and have J. Nagy's room equipped for intensive care. He would even make sure it had only the most up-to-date equipment—as long as Aron would please finish the program.

"Anything else?"

"One small thing. There's an international exhibit of roses opening this afternoon. Send a cameraman out, and tell him to get me about five minutes' worth. I want that five-minute sequence shown on the evening news—when I give the word."

"Fine. Now, may I see some footage?"

"As soon as it's ready."

"And when will that be, if I may ask?"

"The word 'when' does not enter into my calculations."

"But I have to have something to tell the bosses."

"Tell them J. Nagy's doctor has found evidence of impaired circulation."

"Well, that's something at least."

◆　◆　◆

Dear Dr. Tiszai:

Once again I am counting on your support of the arts and taking the liberty of asking your kind patronage.

When I last visited our patient, I could not help but notice that her strength was rapidly waning. If this is actually the case, I must start preparations now for the final scene. I hope I can enlist your cooperation.

You may recall how Mrs. Miko was looking forward to the flower show. Now she will not be able to participate. But I have persuaded the station to do a short feature on it, and if we can show it to her I am certain it will be one of her last joys.

Although I am not familiar with the development of Mrs. Miko's illness, I imagine that sooner or later it will reach a point at which you as a doctor will be able to judge how long she has to live. It would be ideal for me if the denouement were to fall some time between half past seven and eight, during the evening news.

The evening news is put together in the afternoon. I can arrange for the flower show to be included if you notify me *by six* that our patient is nearing death. After six only world events of great importance can be added.

May I therefore request that you contact me at extension 676 by six o'clock should the need arise. I ask you this favor not only in the interest of my film, but in Mrs. Miko's interest as well. I feel there is no finer way for her to take leave of the living.

In the hope of hearing from you soon, I remain,

Yours respectfully,
Aron Korom

♦ ♦ ♦

Dear Mr. Korom,

I have torn your outrageous letter to pieces. Not for a minute will I tolerate so flagrant an infringement of medical ethics in my hospital—not even the suggestion of it.

The fact that you yourself are not a doctor is no excuse. You must know that the Hippocratic Oath requires me to make people well, that is, prolong their lives. I cannot time my patient's death to conform to your artistic imagination or the schedule of the evening news. As far as I am concerned, you never wrote that letter.

You are unfortunately correct, however, in assuming Mrs. Miko's condition to be critical. I am afraid she will not live through tomorrow. Since I still believe in your project, I thought I ought to let you know you must be ready now if you wish to capture the patient's last moments on film. I have already notified her family.

Sincerely yours,
Dr. Istvan Tiszai
Internal Medicine

◆ ◆ ◆

Morning

"How come you didn't call first?"

"We just thought we'd drop by."

"Have you been talking to the doctor?"

"No, no. We just happened to be in the neighborhood."

"Oh. I thought the doctor. . . ."

"No. You're wrong."

"If you're still here when he comes, you can have a talk with him. He comes every day now."

Her voice seemed to have faded since they had seen her last. Her face was skin and bones. A mask.

Yet everything she said had a more hopeful ring to it than before.

"How do you feel?"

"I've stopped eating. All I do is sleep. I'm exhausted."

"Are you in pain?"

"The doctor must be giving me stronger medicine because all I can feel is the tension in my stomach. Or it may just be that the atmosphere here at home is better."

"When did that begin?"

"A few days ago. I've been doing a lot of complaining, haven't I?"

"What's changed?"

"Lots of things. Mama—who never used to lift a finger for me—Mama gives me a washing every morning. She asks me if I want tea or lemonade, brings me my medicine, feeds me my meals. Eight years ago when her glaucoma started acting up, I tried to make her feel better by saying, 'Don't worry. From now on I'll be your eyes.' And you know what? The other day she said to me, 'You're my eyes; I'll be your legs. Tell whatever you need.' She remembered! Isn't that wonderful? And even more important, she's stopped bickering with the Nuofers."

"And all within the last few days?"

"Yes, and high time too. True, they do everything they can to soften her up. Sandor stuffs her with chocolate, and his wife makes bean soup or pork ribs and cabbage just for her. Once I even heard her say, 'Delicious, dear.' She never said anything that nice to me."

"I hope it's set your mind at rest."

"Well, it's come just at the right time, at the last minute. My end is near. I can tell. But I'm not afraid."

"Do you really mean that?"

"I really do."

"But how can you not be afraid? You don't have to answer if you don't want to."

"No, we can talk about it. To tell the truth, I'm more frightened by the thought that my body's going to be closed up in a coffin with a lid on top than by the thought of death. That's the only thing that bothers me about it."

"Do you think you can explain why?"

"I always loved having people around me—the people at the nursery during the day, Mama and a neighbor or two in the evening. It's good being together with people. But once they nail the lid down on that coffin, that's it."

"In other words, the greatest loss you feel is the loss of companionship."

"Yes. That's exactly what I wanted to say."

"So you couldn't imagine living alone."

"Oh no. Not that I got much pleasure out of people. I lived with my husband for six years. It wasn't particularly good or bad, but we belonged together. In fifty-six he got mixed up in the street fighting and began coming home with a machine gun. Then one day he headed for the border. A few months later he sent a message over Radio Free Europe saying he'd made it to America, but I don't even know who it was meant for: I never heard a word from him again. Then Mama's eyes began giving her trouble—I had to come to grips with that. And with the Nuofers moving in. I was never any good at changing anything. And now this. I'll come to grips with this, too. Well, I guess that answers your question."

"What question?"

"About whether I'm afraid. You see, I'm not. The way I am now, that's the way I'll be then. There won't be any difference."

"But you must have *some* pleasurable memories."

"I can't think of any."

"Well, from the way old man Franyo talked, they seemed to value you highly at the nursery."

"You bet they did. Where else would they find a fool like me who did anything anybody asked and did a good job of it, too?"

"What about the roses? Didn't you like the roses?"

"Oh, I'm glad you brought that up. Yes, I loved the roses."

"Tell us something about them."

"About the roses? What do you want me to say?"

"Forget it. It was a silly question."

"You're not silly, *I'm* silly. I've been working with roses for as long as I can remember, and all I can say about them is there's no flower more beautiful in all of Hungary."

"Thank you. That's enough for now. Wouldn't you like to take a rest?"

"I am tired, it's true. But if you need it for your program, we can go on talking for a while."

"No, you go to sleep now. Will it bother you if the two of us stick around?"

"No, of course not."

"We'll be quiet. Sleep well."

♦ ♦ ♦

Afternoon

Mrs. Miko was still asleep. Aron and his cameraman had retreated to a corner, where they sat and waited. Hours passed. Mama would come in from time to time, bend down close enough to her daughter's face to see it, and then go out again. It was dark by the time the Nuofers came home. They put on the light in the kitchen, but did not make a sound. The silence was overpowering. It seemed as though even the buses were doing their best not to disturb Mrs. Miko's sleep.

Finally the doorbell rang. Mrs. Miko woke up. The cameraman went to open the door. Dr. Tiszai had come straight from the hospital. He was still in his white coat. He sent them into the hall for a few minutes while he examined her.

"I just hope we don't miss the news," said Aron.

"Don't worry. We've got twenty more minutes," said the cameraman, who had a watch with a dial that shines in the dark.

The doctor called them back in. "Get everything ready," he whispered. "I'll be staying, too."

Mrs. Miko was awake, but she did not even turn her face in their direction.

"Who's that?" she asked in a voice so weak they could scarcely hear it.

"The TV people."

"Call in Mama and the Nuofers. I want everybody to be here."

"Right away," said Aron. "And if you don't mind, I'll bring in the TV too."

"What for? I'm never going to watch TV again."

"But what if there's something interesting on?"

"Interesting? For me?"

They brought in the set and put it on a chair on the far side of the bed. Then the cameraman led in Mama. He gave her a seat, asked her to stand up again, and found her another seat. He had to make sure she would not block his view of Mrs. Miko. The Nuofers stood in the doorway. Mrs. Miko had tears in her eyes. The cameraman backed into a corner.

"Ready?"

"Ready."

"All right then. I am now turning on the television set," he said turning on the television set.

He and his cameraman stood behind the set, following what was on the screen from the newscaster's patter.

It began with the flood again. Dams fortified with sandbags.

Arabs homeless. Then a new assembly line in the Budapest Tungsram plant. Then a meeting of the Academy of Sciences. And finally! Thank God it wasn't too late.

"And now a report from Budafok, where the first international flower show devoted entirely to roses and the arrangement of roses is just getting under way."

They zoomed in on Mrs. Miko's face as best they could. "My God," she said raising her head and staring at the screen. "My God, it's us! Can you prop me up?"

Dr. Tiszai put his arms around her, lifted her up, and stuffed two folded over pillows behind her back.

"Can all the rest of you see, too?" Her voice was clear now. The rust had been sanded off.

"There's old man Franyo! Just look at all the flags! And look, there they are—the roses! That's the Mephistopheles from Margaret Island. And that's Chevalier Delbord from southern France. Deep red. Why can't your TV do a better job of showing them? And there's the Czardas. It's pink. It comes from Margaret Island too. The yellow Flamenco. The Mysterium—white on the outside, reddish on the inside. I wish they'd do a better job of showing them. There's a Canadian rose, the Ocean Pearl, that goes from yellow to wine-red. It's much more beautiful when you see it in person. And there's the New Europe from Bonn, from Germany. These now are all Swedish. And here comes our turn. The Citronella and the Fairy Princess. That's Mrs. Kantor. She said we should enter the Dying Swan. It would have been much better than what we ended up with. It's all white except for a scarlet Tamango in its side. That was my idea. It's the blood coming from the wound. . . . Who won? We did, didn't we? Where's old man Franyo? Who's that accepting the prize? Never saw him before in my life. I wonder what it would have been like if I'd been there. Well, that's the end. I wish they'd done a better job of showing them, but even so it was good to see what went on. Thank you, boys. Thank you, doctor. Thanks, I'm fine. Thanks, I don't need anything."

The doctor gave her an intravenous injection, but this time he did not bother to send them out of the room. The patient's eyes were open. The blanket moved up and down in time with her breathing. She was still alive, but on her way somewhere, perhaps in toward her stomach, which was as large as a pregnant woman's.

Dr. Tiszai sat down. The camera was still rolling. Nobody moved. Nobody said a word. The minutes passed more and more slowly. The cameraman looked over at Aron, but Aron motioned back to him to keep going no matter how long the silence lasted.*

After a long interval Mrs. Miko finally broke the silence. What she said was more of a sigh than anything else. "Please ask Mama to come in."

"Here I am, Mariska. Is there anything you need?"

No answer. The doctor took the patient's pulse. She was still breathing, but now her breathing was clearly audible. She opened her eyes and stared up at the ceiling. Aron went up to her.

"If you have the least bit of strength left, may I ask you to turn toward your mother?"

Mrs. Miko slowly turned her head in a direction where no one happened to be.

"Is Sandor here, too?"

"Over here," whispered Nuofer.

"Take Mama's hand, please."

"Go and sit down next to her," whispered Aron. "Look at the camera."

Everyone was whispering now. A loud voice would upset the patient. Nuofer sat down next to Mama and took both her hands in his.

"Are you together?" asked Mrs. Miko.

"Yes, we're together," said Mama.

"I'm holding your mother's hands," said Nuofer.

"Can you see me, Mariska?" asked Mama.

---

* This is where they cut in the nursery footage: people walking around and talking interspersed with endless rosebeds. But they showed it without the sound track, like a silent film, so the two silences—in the apartment, in the nursery—seemed to echo one another: the world had been struck dumb. It was one of the finest sequences in the film.

There was no response. For a while nothing happened. Then Mrs. Miko heaved a deep sigh. "She's dead," wailed Mama.

The doctor took Miko's pulse and shook his head. No. Not yet. She's still alive. But Aron signaled to his cameraman. His instinct told him this was it. To keep from getting in the picture, he walked along the wall all the way to the door. The cameraman followed. Then Aron started in the direction of the bed. Like a wedge he parted Mrs. Nuofer and her son, Sandor and Mama. The camera followed him slowly, then stopped, directly in front of Mrs. Miko's face.

Aron's instinct had paid off. The doctor let go of Mrs. Miko's hand, stood up, and nodded twice. Death. There was nothing frightening, nothing awe-inspiring about it. A pair of eyes had closed, a head had fallen to one side, the blanket had stopped moving up and down. Someone who had been was no more. The picture before Mrs. Miko's closed eyes had come to an end much as a sentence comes to an end.

♦ ♦ ♦

On the afternoon of the funeral the sky was overcast. The city was enveloped in a daytime darkness of low floating storm clouds. Suitable lighting for a funeral, perhaps, but not for filming.

The crowd that had gathered at the coffin was so large that Aron thought he had come to the wrong place. Mrs. Miko couldn't possibly have had so many friends and relatives. When he and the camerman finally elbowed their way up to the coffin, an old man in mourning said to them, "Are you sure you haven't made a mistake? This is the funeral of a woman from our nursery."

"Is her name Mrs. Miko?"

"That's right."

"Then we've come to the right place."

Their appearance caused a bit of a stir. The adults, both men and women, stepped aside for them. Only the children dared go up to the camera. Mrs. Miko had been a Protestant. The service began. The young minister, who had not yet delivered many funeral orations, got stage fright in front of the camera. All through the speech his voice kept cracking, and by the end he was completely hoarse.*

The coffin seemed ready to cave in under all the roses. There were so many of them that an entire carful of bouquets and wreaths followed the hearse to the cemetery. Mama's black veil made her more blind than usual, and Aron had to lead her up to the grave.

"Make sure I'm not in the picture," she told him.

"Why don't you want people to see you?"

"Because I can't cry, and the neighbors would talk."

And she did not cry, either during old man Franyo's speech or afterwards, when the first lumps of earth hit the coffin. By that point all the other women were in tears, and even the men were beginning to sniffle. The lens made a leisurely pan of the faces, lingering over each one of them for a moment, drawing up a catalogue of peasant miseries. Then, suddenly, it swept over to the grave.

"Keep her rolling," said Aron to the cameraman, who was now circling slowly over the flowers at short range.

One rose next to another. One rose peeking out through two others. Many roses merging into one. Then a single rose again. And another. And another. And another. And more. "Cut!" said Aron to the cameraman. "What do you think? How's it going to be?"

"Fucking fantastic!" The cameraman was a man of few words.

♦ ♦ ♦

When the mourners began to go their separate ways, Aron went off in search of Mama. She was still standing near the grave—fat, veiled, alone.

---

* They realized right away they would have to throw it out, but luckily the service next door had a Catholic priest with a good rich voice, and they filmed a minute or two of him. As a result, the Protestant Mrs. Miko ended up with a Roman Catholic burial, but at least the funeral oration was loud and clear.

"I've got my car here. Can we take you home?"

"Yes, please do. Obviously nobody cares about me any-more."

They could just about squeeze her into the car. She talked a blue streak all the way, from the moment they set off till the moment they pulled up in front of the house, though that did not stop her from devouring a greasy sausage roll she had bought: the long service made her hungry.

She had very few words to say about her daughter. "The poor thing trusted everybody. She died the way she lived, be-lieving only what she wanted to believe."

On old man Franyo's oration: "How he sang her praises. But if I hadn't had a word with him in time, he would have pocketed all the funeral expenses."

On the congregation of mourners: "That was the whole nursery you saw there. First they work her to death, then they think they can make up for it with a few miserable roses."

And finally on the Nuofers: "Did you see them? All in black. I'm surprised they didn't dye their hair black too. And oh how they cried! Well, of course they cried. A gypsy can turn the tears on whenever he feels like it. Or maybe they were real tears—tears of joy. After all, they figure they've made a good deal. But they have another think coming, believe you me. Mariska's been dead for six days now, and for six days dear old Mama has ceased to exist. All they think about is the boy. And let me tell you—that boy was never meant to live. Ever since he poisoned himself, they can't leave him alone. Now I don't want to say anything bad about him, but just be-tween you and me, when he's studying in the bedroom, I go out into the kitchen, and if he comes in after me and wants to play, I go back into the bedroom. I'm an old woman, I'm half blind, I wander around the apartment without saying a word. And if anybody says anything to me, I make believe I don't hear. They won't have a thing to pin on me, and in the end they'll be the ones who'll break the contract. I won't have to lift a finger.

"Thanks for driving me home. You've done a lot of dam-age, it's true, but you're not bad boys at heart. I'll have you over for dinner some time. Around Christmas, all right? Wait till you see it: the bathroom will be ready, the walls painted. And since I know you like a good meal, I'll have the lawyer lady make you stuffed cabbage and chocolate layer cake. That's one of her specialties. And if you want to do me a favor in return, you can drive me out to the cemetery afterwards. She'll have calmed down by then, poor Mariska. Is this it? Come and help me out. These tiny cars certainly weren't made for me. Well, good-bye, boys. I hope the program turns out all right."

◆ ◆ ◆

The next day there was a message waiting for Aron at the station. Ularik had something urgent to talk over with him. Right away he smelt a rat. And rightly so.

"How are you coming along, my boy? The bosses are very curious."

"They won't have long to wait now."

"They feel they've waited long enough. They want a written report, and I want to see what you have on film."

"We don't have the dubbing done yet. There's no music, no sound. You won't get any idea of the end product."

"You're forgetting I'm an old hand at things like that. Splice together what you have and let's get going."

Soon Ularik, Aron, and the cameraman were sitting in the projection room watching the film. There was a long silence after the lights went up. Aron had goose pimples. It was the silence of the firing squad. Ularik lit up a cigarette and inhaled without a word. For as long as anyone could remember he had not uttered a single word of praise. But now he broke the silence with something that sounded like "Not bad."

Had Aron understood it correctly? Another stretch of silence set in.

"I expected it to be more depressing." And a while later: "What's left?"

"J. Nagy."

"Which means you'll end with his funeral too."

"What else can I do? That's what the program's about."

"And what's he going to die of, poor J. Nagy?"

"A heart attack, presumably."

"Too bad."

"Why? A heart attack has more visual impact than cancer."

"That shows how much you know. But then again how could you possibly know the turns a heart attack can take? If you're lucky, J. Nagy will heave one sigh, and that'll be that. They kept my poor father going for four weeks with one of those pacemakers or whatever they call them. If they do the same to J. Nagy, you can forget about seeing your program on the air. We'd get thousands of complaints."

"All I have is one or two sequences left to shoot."

"I don't mind waiting, but the longer you put it off, the more chance there is it will end up on the shelf."

"I'll take that risk. The mere existence of a work of art gives it meaning."

"If Fellini had said that, I would have taken it to heart, but you—you're just a rank beginner sweating out his first film."

"Every genius started as a rank beginner, Ularik."

"Your self-confidence is very impressive, Aron, but even you can't arrange for J. Nagy to have the kind of heart attack we feel suitable for the television audience."

"J. Nagy believes in what he's doing."

"But he can't *will* the way he's going to die."

"When you really want something, you usually manage to get it."

"Well, best of luck, Aron."

♦　♦　♦

In the evening, when things at the hospital quieted down, J. Nagy would take the contraband phone out of its case, plug it in, dial his friend's number, and have a good long talk with him. First he would report on his state of health, then on the vagaries of hospital life. In return, Aron would fill him in on the latest gossip: what his various female acquaintances were up to and what was going on at the station in general—including his session in the projection room with Ularik. "But don't

62

think anybody's trying to push you," he said quickly. "There's no reason to take Ularik too seriously."

"Unless he's right."

"Ularik? Right about what?"

"I'm afraid I've done myself more harm than good with that intensive care idea."

"But that's the way you wanted it, J. Nagy."

"True, but if you saw what it's like to be in intensive care, you wouldn't take what Ularik said about his father so lightly."

"How does it look, an intensive care unit?"

"Drop by tomorrow, and I'll show you one. By the way, I'm not in the best of shape today."

"What's the matter? Does anything hurt?"

"I feel the same kind of pressure in my chest I felt six years ago."

"You are not just trying to give me a scare now, are you, J. Nagy?"

"Courage, my boy, courage. Though I don't believe the news upsets you in the least."

"But we're old friends, and I'm worried about you. You believe *that,* don't you?"

"We're not friends anymore, Aron. We're just artists."

"One doesn't exclude the other."

"Somewhere along the line we had to make a choice: either we'd go on drinking together or we'd make an honest film together. We chose the film. Come over tomorrow and have a look at your backdrop."

◆　◆　◆

When Aron stepped into the room, he did not know where he was. Even a hospital room has its own style, its own atmosphere. The peace, the order, the whiteness take the patient's mind off his suffering and give him hope for recovery. Now this magic had vanished. The four-bed room had become a two-bed room and taken on the appearance of a power plant control center. It was packed full of all kinds of instruments and monitors. An oxygen tank that looked like an aerial bomb stood waiting in the corner. "Watch out! Don't trip over the wires!" J. Nagy called out.

He really was not in the best of shape. He did not rush up to greet him. He did not even get out of bed. The best he could do was sit up. They brought out the wine and the soda water. He did not particularly feel like drinking either. "That's mine over there," he said pointing to some lemonade. And this was the first time they had seen him unshaven.

"Szilvia will be right here. Take a good look when she leans over me with her stethoscope. You won't regret it."

"Thanks, J. Nagy."

"She's in a vicious mood because she found my phone. She confiscated it right away. You'd better apologize to her."

When Szilvia came in, she nodded coolly and then bent over to examine J. Nagy with her stethoscope. Aron got in quite a long look. Then he changed his expression to penitent and asked her forgiveness for the telephone.

"If I do any forgiving at all, it's because you arranged for this room. There are so few beds in intensive care we have to fight hard to get one for a patient."

"Glad to be of help. *Now* are you willing to talk to me?"

"Now that I have permission, yes. Shall I sit, stand, or. . . ."

"Why not lie down?" said J. Nagy. He received a gentle slap for the suggestion.

The bedtable was covered with flowers (a sure sign that his women had not yet given him up). Aron seated Dr. Freund in front of them.

"May I begin?" asked J. Nagy. "The time has come, dear viewers, to introduce you to Dr. Szilvia Freund, who both practices and teaches medicine. She is sitting here next to me, so you can now see two important characters in our program together: the patient—in other words, yours truly—and the doctor. Our relationship is clear and simple, our roles precisely defined: I will do what I have set out to do; she will do everything she possibly can to keep me alive. And we will both do our best to keep you from being either shocked or bored."

"Excuse me," interrupted Szilvia, "but I am a doctor, and

my only concern is to cure my patient. Let's all hope he'll soon be well."

"Yes, let's, of course. But if I'm not, we're going on with our unwritten script."

"What do you mean? We're in a hospital room, not a studio."

"Maybe so, maybe so. But certainly you won't deny the death agony its dramatic effect. There's too much hardware here for my taste. I don't want technology to upstage our little two character play. Put yourself in the audience's place. What did they tune in for? Technological wonders? No! What they want to see is two human beings using their bare hands to do battle with an invisible enemy."

"But if I disregard the latest medical achievements, I may do you great harm."

"You'd be doing me a great service, Szilvia, if you simply left me alone with death."

"You'll have plenty of time to be alone with death, wait until I'm forced to give up my fight. Why are we talking about this anyway?"

"Because I recently heard of a case in which a patient was kept alive artificially for four weeks, and I don't want that to happen to me."

"That's what we call reanimation. It's only necessary in extreme cases."

"Well, if you use it on me, that's the end of all the work we've put into this program. They'll put it right up on the shelf if they think it will upset our audience."

"And you want me to hand back my diploma instead? Is that what you're telling me?"

"Do you know the joke about the millionaire who went to the police to complain about not being issued a beggar's license?"

"Yes."

"Then why won't you let me die, Szilvia?"

"Stop making jokes and tell me what you want of me."

"A man is alive until he loses consciousness. Let's agree beforehand that the moment I lose consciousness, you will quietly

65

withdraw. You will not try to reanimate me. You will not hook me up to any of your machines. You will allow me to play out my role to its natural end."

"I'm sorry. I can't promise you that."

"But what do you intend to do with me?"

"Exactly what we do with every other patient."

"Even if it looks unappetizing?"

"Even then, if necessary."

"So you'd rather put our program on the shelf?"

"That's right."

At that point somebody called for Szilvia from another room, and the discussion was broken off.

"Look what your little love affair's gotten you into," Aron remarked when they were alone.

But J. Nagy just smiled a self-confident smile. "Don't worry, my boy," he said. "The dying man always has the last word."

Before he had a chance to say what the word would be, Dr. Freund was back. She stood holding the door for two orderlies carrying a patient in on a stretcher. They put the stretcher down and lifted the patient up on to the other bed. Szilvia took his pulse and showed Aron out of the room with a wave of the hand.

"Be back here tomorrow at half past ten on the dot," J. Nagy called after him.

As Szilvia leaned over the new patient with her stethoscope, Aron was able to get in one last look at her spectacular breasts.

♦ ♦ ♦

J. Nagy died the next afternoon. His death was just as he had wished it to be: attractive, cinematic, without the least tinge of the unseemly, without the least bit of intervention by the medical profession. He did in fact have the last word.

The time of death could not be established with any degree of accuracy, because when death set in, he was not attended by anyone. Szilvia was taken up with the patient next door. Aron and his crew had gone back to the station. They would all have sworn he was sleeping the sleep of the just.

Aron did not find out until that evening, when Dr. Freund phoned him. "Do you dare to tell me you didn't notice anything?" she said to him in a voice trembling with rage and despair.

"Notice what?"

"As if you didn't know. You're nothing but a common murderer," she said slamming down the receiver.

It was late by then, but Aron rushed over to the station. He was so unsettled he did not trust himself to drive. He grabbed a taxi, asked for the keys to the lab, found the reel he was looking for, and went straight into the cutting room. He ran the film through twice, and then just sat there in the dark staring at the monitor. Now, of course, the sequence took on a completely different aspect, but as hard as he looked, he could not find the frame that might have made him suspect something. Nowhere did he see a hint that J. Nagy's fat body was at that very moment absorbing a dose of sixty sleeping pills.

True, when they walked in that morning at half past ten, he looked as though he had not had much sleep. He even told them he hadn't slept a wink. But he was known as a chronic insomniac, so no one found anything particularly amiss. Besides, he had asked Dr. Freund's permission to do some filming.

"I'm actually glad to see you this time," she said looking up from her work with the new patient. "See if you can take his mind off things. He's been following our every move here."

So they started setting up—unsuspecting, with a clear conscience. But no, that's not quite right either. First they suggested he have a good sleep and put off the filming till the next day. "No, no. Stick around," he said. "And make sure this screen gets into the picture too."

Not a sign that this interview would end in a man's death.

"Camera. . . . Take one!" said Aron, and they were on their way.

◆ ◆ ◆

The writer's bed was separated from his neighbor's by a screen. The patient was scarcely visible: he was merely the combination source and terminus for a cluster of instruments, tubes, and wires. He lay there unconscious, while flashing dots and dashes on monitors observed and transmitted his vital functions. On his head he wore a mask-like cap, his nostrils had two rubber oxygen tubes coming out of them, both his arms were receiving infusions (one of them was also wound around with a blood pressure cuff), and his wrists and ankles were attached to electrodes. There was a nurse beside his bed keeping an eye on him while Dr. Freund kept her eye on the instruments. It was quiet. The only sound was the patient's wheezing.

"Was *he* the reason you couldn't sleep?" asked Aron motioning in the direction of the screen.

"Nobody got any sleep. He was unconscious when they brought him in, but he's come to several times since then. Once he begged them to let him die, but you can be sure he didn't get anywhere with that. I kept my fingers crossed hoping he'd die on his own. I couldn't take my eyes off him. It was like seeing my own future before me."

"Who is he?"

"An anonymous patient. They picked him up off the street. No papers, no money, dead drunk. Each time he comes to, he throws up. It stinks to high heaven."

"Don't you think we ought to call it a day, J. Nagy? Why don't you take a little rest?"

"No, let's keep going. But do me a favor. If I happen to fall asleep, don't wake me up."

"Of course we won't. I can't see why you feel it's so important to go through with it at all. Has something happened you want to put in the program?"

"The only thing that's happened is, for the first time since I started in with this role—for the first time I'm scared. I always took life easy and figured I could make an easy break with it, more or less the way I used to break off my affairs. And now for the first time I realize there are other ways as well."

"Was it Anonymous over there who gave you the scare?"

"Yes. You've got a real bastard for a friend, you know? They didn't put up the screen until it started to get light, so I saw it all. I tried to tell myself there was no point worrying about him. We were two completely different people, after all. But it didn't work. We aren't different; we have the same fate. The only thing that separates us is the arm's length between our beds. Nothing, nothing at all. *I* might just as well be clinically dead, too."

"But look, they've brought him back to life. Doesn't that make you feel a little better?"

"Not me it doesn't. Granted I've read everything there is to read on the subject, but reading isn't seeing. They opened a vein and threaded a tiny little gadget through it up his arm and into his heart. It's been there ever since, beating his heart for him with electrical impulses. I couldn't get over how elegantly Szilvia slid that crutch into a heart that had already stopped. 'What a gorgeous hangman you are, Szilvia,' I said to her. 'Are you planning to do the same to me?' 'Don't call me Szilvia,' she said, 'and try to get some sleep.' That was when she had the screen brought in. What's she doing now?"

"Just sitting."

"Sitting and waiting to make a mess of our program. Well, let her wait."

"Stop torturing yourself over the program, J. Nagy."

"But I've put so much work into it I want something in return. What if the screen was here instead of there and it was my bed Szilvia was sitting at. You're the director—what would you do with me? The audience doesn't give a damn about a helpless body; what the audience wants is a feeling, thinking human being who looks into the camera, the way I'm doing now, and gives a clear-headed articulate analysis of the situation."

"And that's exactly the way we intend it to be."

"The road to hell is paved with good intentions. No, we can't leave a thing to chance. In other words, what we need is a brainstorm on the part of our director."

"But I have no power over life and death, J. Nagy."

"Why don't you just admit you can't come up with anything?"

"What do you want me to come up with anyway? *You* put

yourself in the hospital; *you* went after Szilvia Bigbreasts; *you* had the intensive care unit brought in. You made your bed, now lie in it. Or even better—go to sleep in it."

"Well, I have the solution, the only solution. I hit upon it this morning when I was really down."

"What is it?"

"It's twice as much work, but it'll pay off in the end. Listen closely. Instead of dying once, I'm going to die twice. Why are you staring at me like that? It's as simple as ABC. First I'll do a death agony that even Ularik will approve of, and then if things work out, you can get the real one on film too. Which means you'll have two deaths to splice together in any way you see fit."

"But that's dishonest, J. Nagy. We're making a documentary film."

"For the shelf or for an audience?"

"You were the one who told me to shoot it as it came and not try to artsy it up."

"I bet you my first death will be better than the real one."

"Well, it doesn't cost anything to try. And now that we're this far along, we might as well. The only trouble is, you're a writer, not an actor."

"Don't worry your head about that, my friend. Even if I were an actor, I couldn't deliver a line I didn't believe. Fortunately, I've done so much thinking about death lately, I'm as close to it as I am to you."

"Are you in any pain?"

"No, not at the moment."

"You *will* have to lie if the only thing wrong with you now is that you're sleepy."

"Isn't that enough? In fact, let's start right there. We'll call being sleepy the threat of death. Remember, I was a bad sleeper all my life."

"I know."

"Now, what else do we need? I know. Why not say I've just poisoned myself."

"I don't understand. How could you poison yourself, J. Nagy?"

"Simple: sleeping pills. They're certainly easy enough to come by. Figure it out for yourself. Every night the nurse puts two sleeping pills on my bedtable. Sixty pills is the mortal dose. Now let's say that for the good of the film I'd resolved to give up sleep. Let's say I'd already taken the sixty pills. And let's say I took them fifteen minutes before you got here. Look at me as if I had only fifteen more minutes of life left in me. There's nobody here to bother you. Szilvia can't see or hear us: she's all wrapped up in Anonymous. Incidentally, what's going on over there?"

"She's talking to two men in white."

"Fine. That means a conference, and a conference means the doctors have come to a stalemate. Let's get this show on the road. *A Writer Bites the Dust*. Take one."

"What do you want me to do?"

"Ask questions."

"What kind of questions?"

"Any kind at all. Whatever we say will seem tragic on the screen. Let's just get it down on film before the conference is over."

"All right. J. Nagy's death. Take one."

♦ ♦ ♦

"Our viewers, I am sure, join me in welcoming you back, J. Nagy. Here we are in the hospital room where you have been confined for some time now. My first question is: How do you feel?"

"Neither particularly good nor particularly bad. The tests indicate my heart is beginning to fall down on the job though."

"What about your general condition?"

"My head is clear, but I'm quite sleepy. My limbs feel weighted down, and I'm having trouble moving my tongue."

"Shall I get you a cup of coffee?"

"I don't have much time left. Let's not waste it."

"Now that we're on the subject of time, let me ask you this. The rest of us think in terms of years or decades. Can you give

71

us an idea of what it feels like to have only a few minutes left?"

"Oh, it's not so bad. You can have a good ten minutes just as you can have a bad thirty-five years. And there's one advantage I have over everybody else: I can't ruin my life anymore."

"Ever witty, I see. But people aren't watching *this* program for your sense of humor."

"Not even if it's gallow's humor?"

"Let's try to be a little more serious now, shall we? Good. Tell us, how do you plan to spend the rest of your time?"

"First I'd like to have something to drink. My throat is beginning to feel parched."

He took a gulp of his lemonade.

"Mm, that was good," he said contentedly. "What I'm planning to do—was that what you asked? If I smoked, I'd light up one last cigarette. If I were a great author, I'd deliver an appeal to mankind. If I were still a man and could be alone with Szilvia, I'd pull her under the covers with me and hope to hell I could get it up."

The cameraman began to laugh. Someone behind the screen told them to keep the noise down. Aron was furious.

"First you rush me into this, and then all you can come up with is the kind of crap you *know* Ularik will make me cut."

"That's Ularik's problem, not mine. Nobody's written a word about the effect of imminent death on sexual potency in the male. It's an important issue, after all."

"But one we can't resolve here. So let's change the subject. And clean up the language too. What are your fondest memories, J. Nagy?"

"Women."

"And what has caused you the most pain?"

"Women again."

"Quit it, will you, J. Nagy! If you go on like this, your death agony will end up the main attraction in a New Year's Eve nightclub act."

"Ask a silly question, you get a silly answer. How about coming up with something better."

"All right then. If you were to die in the next few minutes, would you be afraid? And please, this is no joke. I want a serious answer."

"Well, I wish you wouldn't go switching into the conditional like that. How do you expect me to stay in character? You must assume that the pills have begun to go to my head by now."

"If that's the way you want it. Then let me ask you, in the good old present tense, whether you want Dr. Freund to pump your stomach for you."

"No, I don't."

"So you're *not* afraid."

"No, I'm not."

"Can you give us any explanation? Both our viewers and I would be very interested, because *we* are all afraid of death."

"The thing is, while I was getting ready for this program, I had a lot of time to think about death. Death has the upper hand—we all know that. Every minute we call our own really belongs to death. Every minute of every hour of every day. What we don't know is which one it's going to choose. That's why you're all afraid of death. But I've outwitted death. Before long I'm going to fall asleep the way I used to when I put down my book, turned out the light, and closed my eyes. In a few minutes I'm going to go through the daily routine one more time. In other words, I've given death the slip. For the first time in my life I'm free."

"Thank God. A little philosophy at last. The only problem is, your voice is sounding a little weak."

"All this talking is wearing me out. If you move the mike a little closer, you can still get in a few more questions."

"Then let me ask you, J. Nagy, whether these minutes of freedom have been worth the price of never waking up again."

"So what if I never see this hospital room again or Anonymous over there, or Ularik or Aranka or Iren. Will the world be any worse off without a second-rate writer and a documentary on air pollution? And think what it's getting instead: a film where for the first time in human existence an artist robs death of its jealously guarded secrets. You'll have to admit that

73

everybody comes out on top this way. You asked whether I was afraid. You can't be afraid if you have nothing to lose."

"But there is one thing you can lose, J. Nagy. The distinction between being and non-being."

"Yes, that's true."

"Well, what are your thoughts on that subject? We're interested in anything you might come up with."

"You still remember a little arithmetic, don't you? Well, J. Nagy minus J. Nagy equals nothing. And nothing will come of nothing."

"Cut it out, will you, and answer my question. You're wasting valuable time. I didn't ask you about nothingness, I asked you about annihilation. There is a common belief that animals can feel death coming, and when they feel it coming for them, they run and hide. What do *you* feel going on inside yourself several minutes before 'annihilation'? Take a good, deep look and tell us what you find."

"Tell you what I find? I find your voice seems farther and farther away."

"Tell us about yourself, not my voice."

"But I don't notice anything special."

"Pull yourself together, J. Nagy. We're almost out of film. This is your big moment. Concentrate."

"What the hell do you want me to concentrate on?"

"Tell us whether you feel at one with yourself at this critical point in your life."

"I do."

"And is the feeling entirely harmonious or the result of a struggle? Is it lying there peacefully or about to explode? Say something."

"If what you're asking is whether I feel any stress, the answer is no. I'm just going to walk out a door. That's it."

"You make it sound as though you were on your way to the kitchen to make dinner."

"And what's wrong with that?"

"You ought to be ashamed of yourself. Is that all you have to offer at the climax of your career? I hope you realize I'm going to have to cut this whole section."

"Why? I think my death is coming along just fine."

"But it's so boring, J. Nagy! How can the viewer get involved if he doesn't feel something valuable will be lost when you go? The least you could do is put up a fight. Even a fly goes through contortions before it dies. Come on, J. Nagy. Give us a conflict."

"I'm doing the best I can."

"Well, it's not enough. I'm surprise at you, J. Nagy. If that's all you have to offer, then the only thing left is to think up some effective farewell."

"Farewell?"

"Farewell to the world."

"I'm getting more and more sleepy now, Aron."

"That's too bad, but no farewell scene—no program. The first thing people want to know when somebody dies is what his dying words were."

"My mind's a blank."

"Force yourself."

"I can hardly keep my eyes open."

"You've got to."

"How about if I lay a fart? I was always better at farting than at writing."

"*Another* stupid joke. Look, we're going to pack up and go home if you don't start behaving yourself."

"All right, all right. You can cut the bit about farting. Now, where were we?"

"The audience would like to hear the dying writer's last words."

"I can't think of anything."

"Try hard, J. Nagy. You've been thinking about nothing else for weeks."

"But thoughts depend on a given situation. What seemed important to me then seems a soap bubble to me now."

"Can't you even come up with one well formulated sentence?"

"Everything I felt so sure of till now has lost its value."

"Well improvise then."

"Maybe the best thing for me to do is just say good-bye to

you. Good-bye, Aron. I hope you make a lot more good programs."

"Cut the hearts and flowers, will you? Remember what you once said? We're professionals."

"Even a professional can be sleepy."

"That's no excuse. Now back to work. We have to give the audience *something* after all."

"Look, my life has been one long headache. Can't you let me die in peace?"

"Only shopkeepers die in peace, and television stations don't send out teams to film them. You're a writer. Your audience respects you. They're hanging on your every word."

"What do you expect me to do? Pick something out of the blue? Tell lies? I don't have the strength left for that kind of thing."

"Say whatever you like. Just make it beautiful. Beauty is art, and art can't lie."

"All art is a lie, Aron."

"A lie people can have faith in."

"Faith? In what? The eternal compromise?"

"You take that back! And fast!"

"I will not."

"Then that's the end of our program."

"That's fine with me. I'm finished. I'm going to sleep. Good night, Aron."

"You can't do this to me, J. Nagy. Just make one big last effort, and try to speak more clearly. This isn't the way a writer dies."

"Oh, yes it is."

"Maybe your memory is failing you because you're so sleepy. Well, let me help you remember. You not only agreed to the role, you've worked on it for weeks. You can't tell me you've lost faith in it all. Now, at the last minute."

"No, I still believe in it. For the first time in my life I'm doing work that doesn't require me to lie."

"You're just saying that because it sounds good."

"Wait and see, Aron. You'll understand some day, too. Nothing in the world is genuine but death."

"Finally! See, you did have it in you! Do you think you could turn a little toward me?"

"No."

"Too bad. But it's better than nothing. Those will be your dying words. Now say them again, will you? More clearly."

"What?" asked the writer listlessly.

"What you just said. But stop winking and blinking and look up at the camera. What's the matter? Have you forgotten it? You said there was nothing in the world that was genuine but death. Come on now, repeat it after me. And open your eyes if you can."

There was no response.

"Open your mouth, J. Nagy! Just spit it out, and then you can do what you like."

Once again no response. The cameraman went up to the bed.

"Hey, Aron," he said. "He's asleep."

Aron got up to have a look.

"What are we going to do now?" he sighed. "Do you think that damn sentence will come through at all?"

"It may."

The writer heard none of this. He had completely succumbed to sleep. Now Aron almost felt sorry for him. He shouldn't have tortured him so. What did they expect from him anyway? He hadn't slept the whole night, poor thing. Now the peace of the fat man settled over his features. He had looked so haggard a few minutes ago. And the hint of a smile that now played on his lips suggested one last punchline on its way.

Aron motioned to the cameraman. The last shot of the writer showed him napping peacefully against a background of the screen and the bedtable with the flowers and lemonade glass.

That done, they began packing up—careful not to make a sound.

♦ ♦ ♦

"Quick, the respirator," said Szilvia to the nurse, who rolled a modern looking piece of equipment over to the patient's bed.

Aron and the cameraman stopped to let her go by and found themselves trapped. A captive audience, they watched Szilvia lower a tube with a little light at the end into the patient's mouth, down his windpipe, and into his lung. Who knew what it would do there. If that was a respirator, maybe it would start the patient breathing again. He needed something all right: his face was almost as white as his pillow. J. Nagy would know for sure. But luckily, he was asleep. It would just have gotten him all worked up again.

"Is it functioning?" asked the nurse.

"Yes, fine," said Szilvia. And for the first time she realized Aron and the cameraman were there. "What are you waiting for?"

"J. Nagy is asleep. He asked not to be awakened."

"I'm glad," said Dr. Freund, without taking her eyes off Anonymous. "It's better if he doesn't watch us."

She stepped aside. Finally they were free to go. Take a deep breath. Run down the stairs. Get into their car. Drive back to the station.

"Well, what do you think?" Aron asked on the way there.

"He wasn't in good form today," replied the cameraman.

"I told him we needed an actor instead of a writer."

"Right," concluded the cameraman.

Aron took the reel up to the lab the minute they arrived. He wrote RUSH on it without realizing it was the last reel of the program.

◆　◆　◆

The station regarded J. Nagy as their own casualty. "He died a hero," said Ularik in his funeral speech, "in the line of duty. His memory will live on in the hearts of our viewers."

As was only right and fitting, a throng of beautiful women crowded around J. Nagy's grave. Aron Korom was nowhere to be seen. His friends had advised him that, considering the prevailing mood, he would do best to stay away.

◆ ◆ ◆

*The Flower Show**

The Flower Show made a gloomy, depressing, but thoroughly thought-provoking television program. The goal of its authors was to give the audience a look into the bourne from which, as the saying goes, no traveler returns.

The three main characters, whom we accompanied on their final journeys from sickbed to grave, gave magnificent performances. Director Aron Korom did a good job as well, though at times the novelty of the assignment proved too much for him: this was his first film.

Special kudos to Hungarian Television for making the film a reality. Thanks to the television camera we can plumb the oceans' depths, climb the Himalayas, probe the secrets of the virgin forests—and all in the comfort of our own living rooms. In other words, we have achieved the impossible. People today know more of the world than ever before. "But there isn't any model for death," says one of the characters in the program. The authors of *The Flower Show* now filled this gap. Even the most discriminating viewer, the viewer who demands edification as well as entertainment, can feel he spent a memorable hour in front of the screen.

The program that followed, *A Visit to a Ninety-Five-Year-Old Miller,* provided an effective contrast. Its high-spirited title character, still on the job, reminded us that death is only part of life and that if we keep healthy and avoid harmful influences we can prolong this beautiful life we all love so dearly.

* A review from the daily press.

THE TOTH FAMILY

Translated by Clara Gyorgyey

*When a snake devours itself
(a rare phenomenon) is there a
snake-size gap left in the world?
And is there a power mighty
enough to make a man devour his
humanity to the last crumb? Is
there or is there not? It's quite a
puzzle!*

Postcard from the front:

My Dear Parents and Agi,

Yesterday I learned that Major Varro, our beloved company
commander, had been granted a ten-day leave because of his
poor health. As soon as I heard this, I went to him and tried to
convince him to take advantage of your hospitality instead of
going to his brother's hot and noisy city apartment. At first, he
didn't want to accept my invitation: he thought his delicate nervous state would be a burden to you. He has in fact been suffering from insomnia for some time now—the partisan raids have
upset him terribly—and he is also extra-sensitive to smells: some
odors he simply can't tolerate, while others, such as the scent of
pine trees, relax him. Fortunately, I remembered that his brother's flat was near a rendering plant, so I went back to him and
described our house at Matraszentanna, our spacious yard with
its view of Mt. Babony, and our sweet, tranquil valley redolent
of pine. Well, to make a long story short, he has accepted my
invitation! He is planning to leave the beginning of next week,
provided, of course, that the partisan attacks taper off. You can't
imagine how important this is for me! The furlough train leaves
from Kursk, and he told me I could ride to the station with him.
Thank God, in the city I'll finally be able to take a bath!

CHAPTER ONE

Matraszentanna is a small mountain town, so small, in fact, that it has no indoor plumbing. Anyone wishing an inside flush toilet has to install his own private pump. Only Professor Cipriani, the proud owner of the town's one mansion, could afford such a luxury. The rest of the population have to make do with their outhouses.

The Toths, for example, like everyone else in town, had only a simple outhouse. One day a putrid smelling watercart stopped in front of the Toth house. The cesspool cleaner jumped down from his seat and hooked his pump to the rubber pipe sticking out from under the wooden fence and extending under blooming hollyhocks to the outhouse in the back yard.

"Shall I pump or not?" asked the cesspool cleaner as Lajos Toth walked toward him.

"That depends on whether it stinks enough to make it worthwhile," replied Toth. "I'm too used to it. I leave that decision up to you, my dear doctor."

The man took several deep breaths with his eyes closed and at last said, "To be perfectly honest, the overall smell of the Toth outhouse is slightly pungent, but by no means unpleasant."

"If there's any smell, let's pump," said Toth. "Don't forget, dear doctor, our son's life depends on it!"

The cesspool cleaner had a Ph.D. in law from the university but could make twice as much money as a cesspool expert than he could as a lawyer.

"It's not so easy to make the right decision in this business," he said still sniffing the air with a pensive expression. "Let's suppose I start pumping. What happens then? The mass down there gets stirred up, and even if I emptied the whole septic tank, I'd pollute the air rather than improve it. As long as the old pulp remains undisturbed, the nice filmy layer on top prevents the escape of any excessive odor. . . ."

"Then what should we do, dear doctor?"

"In my opinion, we must choose the lesser of the two evils. The real question is, exactly how sensitive is the major to smells? What did your son say?"

"Our Gyula wrote that the major was very sensitive."

"What makes you think that this particular odor will irritate him?"

"Oh, we once had a tenant who complained about it," said Toth with concern, "and he wasn't even a major, just a sleeping-car attendant."

"Let me be frank," said the watercart owner after a brief silence. "I never lie to my old customers, especially when the risk is so great. The fact of the matter is that after a thorough pumping, completely odor-free air (if such a thing exists at all) cannot be expected for four or five weeks minimum. Do you have that much time until your guest arrives?"

"He is scheduled to arrive on the first furlough train."

"In that case, I think it would be wiser not to do anything."

"Thank you very much for your valuable advice," responded Toth. "Now then, what do I owe you?"

"Nothing, my good man," replied the watercart owner. "I charge only for pumping; consultations are free."

The first bus from Matraszentanna to Eger leaves at 5:30 A.M. but there are two later ones at 1:20 and 6:00 P.M. Mrs. Toth took the second bus to the city and rushed straight to the Apollo Cinema. She found the foyer empty. The only person to be seen was a bald man seated in the cashier's booth. She assumed he must be Mr. Aszodi, the owner.

"Excuse me, please. Are you Mr. Aszodi by any chance?"

"I am. And who are you?"

"Well, a while back, when Mr. Berger owned the theater, I used to be the cleaning lady."

"Don't talk so loud," scolded the proud proprietor. The show was on and, because of the heat, the doors were half-open. "Are you by any chance, Mrs. Toth, Mariska?"

"Yes, I am. Mariska Toth."

"They had nothing but praise for you," the new owner whispered.

"I'm so glad to hear that. I worked for Mr. Berger for over twelve years as both cook and cleaning lady. The missus ate only kosher food, but he preferred French cooking."

"Do you want to come back to work for me?" inquired the new owner. "Our woman is afraid of the dark."

"Not just now," Mariska said. "I only do washing nowadays. Besides, we're expecting a guest, my son's commanding officer. That's why I'm here. I have a great favor to ask of you, Mr. Aszodi. Would you be kind enough to lend us your vaporizer?"

"What is that? A steam engine?"

"No sir. When I used to work for Mr. Berger, we used it to freshen the air."

"You mean it gives off a scent?"

"Yes, and we need it now," said Mariska. "For the two weeks our guest stays, we have to produce a pine smell in the house."

"I'm not sure we still have it. Of course you may take it if we do," said the theater owner.

"We used to keep it on the spiral staircase leading to the projection room."

"Help yourself, my dear lady. But be careful, the stairs squeak."

Mariska tiptoed up the stairs. The vaporizer was hanging where it always had.

One of the main sources of people's income in Matraszentanna has always been renting rooms to tourists, but unfortunately the State Tourist Bureau recently gave the town only a fair-to-low rating, citing the poor quality of the drinking water and the lack of proper plumbing. As a result, only low-income families, simple white-collar workers and retirees now frequented the place during the tourist season, and to be visited by a bona fide major, irrespective of war time, was a once in a lifetime opportunity.

This was the third summer of the war, and Mrs. Toth's son was not the only local man serving at the front. At least sixty percent of the population had relatives in the armed forces. The arrival of the major had provoked an almost superstitious sense of anticipation in the townspeople, as if the mere presence of so illustrious a military guest would guarantee the safety of every soldier son.

Agi, however, did not know this. She wasn't even quite sure what a major was. She thought the local fire chief was the highest ranking soldier in the world. At any rate, she was at that delicate age (she had just turned sixteen) when girls are afraid of nothing more serious than being made to look foolish.

"Please, don't get mad, but you really can't ask me to do that," she would say to her mother.

The town's inhabitants often helped one another with the tourists. Mrs. Toth, who was overwhelmed with housework, had prepared a list of things to be borrowed from different people. Agi was supposed to do the collection: a bedspread with Chinese design from the Kasztriners, pudding dishes from the Pastor of Tomaji, a few boxes of gelatine from Professor Cipriani's cook, and so on. But how could a mother expect a senstitive young lady to go out begging for such ridiculous items, pulling a little toy cart to put them in! No loving mother could possibly ask her own child to so demean herself.

That was how matters stood when Toth arrived home.

"What is the problem, Agi?" he asked her calmly.

Agi blushed. Whenever her father wore his red fireman's helmet, his overpowering, giant stature and calm patient glance made all her problems shrink into insignificance.

"Nothing in particular," she said. "I was just going to help Mother."

Without any further protest she grabbed the handle of the

toy wagon and started off reluctantly in the direction of her first stop. The first family Agi visited, the Kasztriners, made a great fuss when she gave them her mother's message.

"And who is this guest you want the bedspread for?"

"Some soldier," replied Agi, stepping back as if to demonstrate how she planned to keep him at a distance.

"What kind of soldier?"

"Some major."

"What! A real major in your house!"

"He is Gyula's commander."

"Good Lord!" screamed the dumbfounded Mrs. Kasztriner, who had not only a son but a nephew at the Soviet front. "Tell me everything from the beginning!"

It was early in the morning when Agi set out on her errands, late afternoon when she finally returned home. As her toy cart was piled higher and higher with the borrowed objects, Agi's spirit sank lower and lower. But soon she attracted more and more interest. She had to recite the great news over and over again. The neighbors were so excited they almost tore the poor girl to pieces. At each house she was stuffed with assorted delicacies. At each house her story became a little more colorful and soon she was quite carried away by her own recital. The major, who had originally sent shivers down her spine, became more charming by the hour and began to resemble her beloved father. He was as powerful, tall, and dashing as Chief Toth. He also walked proudly, with dignity. And how brave, generous, and chivalrous he was! A truly exceptional man! Yes, his generosity was legendary; money held no fascination for him; his soldiers idolized him as much as the Russians feared him; they fled panic-stricken into the woods when they heard his name: in sum, a hero!

By the time she reached the end of her route, Agi was so overwrought that she couldn't bear the thought of going home. Instead, she pushed her cart through the gate into her yard and continued to walk to the point where the road curves and the houses end. There she found a spot where the view was perfect: she could see across to the wood-covered peak of Mt.

Babony and the little tranquil valley of Bartalapos. Suddenly the wind seemed to blow, and Agi stretched her burning body on the grass, placed her hands on her rounding breasts, and sensuously massaged them accompanied by the velvety strokes of the gentle breeze. With her eyes wide open, she whispered to herself in a state of intoxication, "An officer! An officer!"

Telegram:

WE REGRET TO INFORM YOU THAT YOUR SON EN-SIGN GYULA TOTH 8–117 HAS FALLEN IN COMBAT STOP HE DIED A HERO'S DEATH STOP THE HUNGAR-IAN RED CROSS.

Matraszentanna's only mailman had been drafted at the on-set of the war. He was replaced by a hunchback—a retarded, stuttering half-wit, whom everyone called Uncle Gyuri.

Uncle Gyuri's only health problem was lack of balance, se-vere lack of balance. While delivering the morning mail, he would walk along in the center of the street on an imaginary line, and became extremely indignant if anyone disturbed the symmetry of his route. He furiously kicked all items lying in his way. If an over-anxious citizen dared to step out on the road to pick up his mail, he would be punished by not receiv-ing his mail until the following day.

When Uncle Gyuri reached the artesian well, he bent down and checked to see that his image was looking back at him from the exact center of the well. People often scolded him and chased him away; everybody assumed he was spitting in the water. That was not true. He was merely discharging a fine, silk-thin thread of saliva from his mouth which—as soon as his lips succeeded in suspending it over the center of the well—he sucked right back into his mouth. This procedure appar-ently refreshed him.

Thus, it was Uncle Gyuri's strange sense of symmetry that determined who would receive mail on any given day. He hated Professor Cipriani, the world famous psychiatrist, whose car often stood on the side of the main street in front of his mansion, thereby destroying the intrinsic balance of the road. But as much as he hated the professor, he loved the Toth family, and most of all Lajos Toth himself.

In fact, it might be said that Uncle Gyuri was in love with the fire chief. Of course, it's common knowledge that shabby people consider those in uniform to be superhuman creatures, much as the infirm revere those who have perfect bodies. But it was more than that for Uncle Gyuri. Lajos Toth was an extremely fastidious man. No one had ever seen him with his helmet tilting to either side or with handkerchiefs dangling out of his pockets. In the eyes of Uncle Gyuri, he was the epitome of human symmetry. Toth even had his hair parted exactly down the middle. As a matter of fact, if someone were to decide to cut Toth in half, he would only have to slice straight down from the part and Toth would fall divided into two identical halves—a rare occurrence even among eggs.

Thanks to Uncle Gyuri, the Toths received only good news from the front, though in fact up to this point he had found it necessary to destroy only one postcard from Gyula—the account of nothing more serious than a mild case of sausage poisoning. The windows of Matraszentanna's post office faced a well-trimmed back yard. Beneath the central window, about an arm's length from the desk, stood an old rain barrel, filled to the brim. Its contents had thickened into jelly-like gutter water, green with age and algae. Every day, after a thorough scrutiny, Uncle Gyuri dropped all letters he found unworthy of delivering into the barrel.

The telegram from the Red Cross bringing the tragic news of Gyula's death ended up there next to a gilded invitation from the Governor inviting Dr. and Mrs. Cipriani to attend a garden party. With one toss the professor received his just desserts and the kind Toths were spared some extremely unpleasant news. The balance of the world had been restored.

At noon, when Uncle Gyuri met the fire chief walking along the street, he gave him an encouraging wink as if to say: "Don't worry, my good friend, as long as I'm around no bad news can reach you and your lovely family." His jolly face caught Toth's attention.

90

"And what makes you so cheerful today, Uncle Gyuri?" he asked.

"What's not good today will be even less so tomorrow!" replied the mailman cryptically, punctuating this wisdom with a distorted grin.

"Anything new otherwise?"

"Otherwise, all is well, sir!"

Toth treated him to a glass of wine. They drank and toasted the health of the heroic Ensign, Gyula Toth. . . .

Matraszentanna is a remote mountain town not normally frequented by majors. One glorious late July morning, however, not one, but incredibly enough, two majors stepped off a bus from Eger.

The first jumped from the still moving vehicle: an erect, elegant character, impeccably dressed, with a manner that immediately commanded respect. A more major-like major could scarcely be imagined. He suited the Toth's image of their son's major to a T.

They found it strange, however, that he did not even look around, but, with a self-assured stride, set off for the Klein Beer Garden next to the railway station.

"Major, sir!" yelled Toth, but the man didn't turn. They finally caught up with him at the entrance to the beer garden and pressed around him at once. Gaping with adoration, they stood there silently as the gentleman barked at them in a brisk, unfriendly manner, "Why are you bothering me?"

"Honorable Major, sir," Toth said. "I am Mr. Toth."

"That's very nice. Now what do you want from me?"

The fire chief winked meaningfully and shoved his daughter toward the officer.

"We welcome you, honorable Major, sir, and from the bottom of our hearts wish you a restful stay in our humble abode." Agi blurted out quivering with stage fright as she awkwardly handed him a bouquet of red roses.

"You've obviously confused me with someone else," said the major, quite irritated. "I am on my way to the officer's rest home in Matraszentmiklos, and only now do I see that this is Matraszentanna. Good-bye."

He turned and trotted off toward an approaching bus, taking the roses with him.

The Toths stared at one another for a moment, stupefied, then rushed back to the bus depot.

The other major, who *had* to be their major, was standing there waiting.

Toth felt a mild pang of disappointment. How could such a short man be a major? Not only was he shorter than the other but shabbier as well. Dressed in a weather-beaten uniform, cracked and dirty boots, and a dusty cap faded by the sun, he was leaning against the artesian well, looking haggard and exhausted. Only Agi displayed any enthusiasm, although she, too, preferred the other major; but this rugged man simply fascinated her. The grease spots on his cape were like blood stains to her, and she gazed at the cape as if it were a bullet-torn military flag, a genuine war relic. She felt like kissing it in patriotic reverence.

Following the awkward greetings and general introductions, Toth began to apologize for the delay, but the major paid no heed. With a nonchalant wave of the hand he dismissed the mix-up, even though it is common knowledge that high-ranking officers are extremely sensitive.

But just when the family began to feel a trifle more relaxed, another misunderstanding clouded the bright sky of the joyous, long-awaited meeting.

Although the major spoke in a rather hoarse voice—indeed, it sounded as if all the dust and dirt of his long trip had settled in his vocal chords—his words were perfectly clear. All he said was, "I never would have thought your charming daughter was so grown-up."

The members of the Toth family were horrified—what all three of them thought they heard rather than the major's polite statement was, "What I want to know is whose breath smells so foul!"

They froze, mortified. Toth was the most shocked because he felt that the major was referring to him. He could think of nothing to say, so he simply held his breath to prevent the offending odor from escaping.

To understand the Toths' anxiety you have to remember how hard they had all worked to make the house smell nice. They had planted hollyhocks around the outhouse, aired the house for a whole day, and sprayed pine scent in every corner with the vaporizer. And after all these meticulous and painstaking preparations Lajos Toth, former railroad worker and current fire chief, well-known for his finely honed mind and sober judgment, had sat down and eaten his customary breakfast: a glass of whiskey and three pieces of garlic bread.

His wife and daughter glared at him in horror. Following their glances, the major also stared at Toth. The fire chief was blushing, his eyes protruded somewhat and his forehead glistened with sweat.

"Aren't you feeling well, my dear sir?" the major inquired politely.

"My husband is upset because he ate garlic bread for breakfast," explained Mariska.

The major studied the fire chief from head to toe and said, "Look, my friends, my nerves have been severely strained by nine months at the front. I've had to bear the brunt of partisan guerrilla tactics. There is no need to explain it all to you, but let me give you one example so you have some idea of what I've gone through."

What followed was a minute description of a pig slaughter. The partisans had ambushed his men, stolen a pig, and very nearly butchered the entire regiment.

The two women listened spellbound to the tale, but the master of the house showed no interest whatsoever. His lack of interest was apparent even to the major.

"Did my story bore you, Mr. Toth?"

Toth said nothing, but his face turned a bit more purple and his eyes shone glassily.

"Of course not!" interjected Mariska.

"All we hear is the front this, the front that," said Agi with glittering eyes, "but until now we've had no idea what was really happening."

"Madame, why is your husband's face turning purple and why doesn't he say anything?"

"Because he doesn't dare breathe out his garlicky breath!" said Mariska.

"Start breathing! On the double!" ordered the major.

As soon as Toth began breathing regularly, his eyes returned to their sockets.

"Please don't let anything like that happen again!" warned the major. "I want you all to ignore my condition. I'm highly disciplined and perfectly capable of controlling myself. By the way, what's that over there? Right behind you, Mr. Toth," he asked suddenly.

"Klein's Beer Garden and the rectory."

"Ah! Good," said the major considerably relieved. Then he told them he didn't wish to be a burden on the family, and the minute he thought he was, he would leave. He asked them not to pay any special attention to him. And while he spoke, he kept looking nervously back over his shoulder.

"Tell me, Toth, do you see anything out of the ordinary behind my back?"

"Nothing whatsoever, sir."

"But you keep looking that way."

"I'm only looking at you, sir."

"Listen, Toth," exclaimed the major, "it's bad enough that half of the world is behind my back. Please don't aggravate the problem by staring there all the time!"

A short silence ensued. The family stood immobile. They did not quite understand what the major's complaint was about; all they could see was that although the street was empty (it was lunchtime) he kept turning toward it. What could be the trouble? Mariska wondered. Her only concern was to provide the best possible care for her esteemed guest: one insulting remark or unpleasant memory might cost her son his life. . . . This realization further intensified her anxiety, and by now she was so upset that even an irksome speck of dust in the major's eye would make her cry. . . . She'd better not let things get out of hand.

"Be a little more careful where you look, Lajos!" she said.

94

"Where do you want me to look?" yelled the indignant fire chief.

"Wherever you please!" came the curt, distant reply from the major. "I make no demands, no special requests, dear Toth."

If these words were meant to reassure Toth, they failed; he was past soothing. When the cause of the trouble is unknown, it is hard to find a cure for it. At first Toth kept his eyes down, then he looked up at the sky; he even tried to shift his body position. But none of these gestures proved satisfactory; they were only half solutions. By now the major didn't only turn his head back and forth, he twisted his whole body around. Eventually everything was behind his back.

When adult logic fails, children may save the situation. "May I say something?" Agi brightly chirped in her refreshing voice. "If Papa would pull his helmet down over his eyes just a wee bit, then it won't make any difference which way he looks."

"Are you out of your mind? Never!" snapped the fire chief.

"At least consider it, dear Lajos," begged Mariska.

The town regarded the helmet as the most prominent feature of a fireman's uniform; it boasted a copper plate engraved with the proud slogan "TOWN FIREMAN," and underneath the brim was a shiny visor to protect its wearer's eyes from sparks. According to the official handbook of the Fire Brigade Association of Northern Hungary, a fireman's body in upright position and the helmet's horizontal axis had to be continually maintained at a precise ninety-degree angle. Of course, Lajos Toth was not the type to bicker about rules and regulations at such crucial moments; he was only afraid of being made to look ridiculous. Deep in his heart he merely wanted to protect his reputation.

He had always enjoyed unequivocal town-wide respect. Before he was appointed fire chief, the town had been sarcastically referred to as "the fire trap" by everybody in the district. What is more, his predecessor—a puny, excitable, ambitious, and over-zealous fireman—never stopped badgering the populace. He had held random fire drills day and night, ordered impossible safety measures implemented, and fined anyone who tossed his cigarette butt in the street. And the end result?—one devastating fire after another.

Lajos Toth did not follow his predecessor's example. He was a born fireman; his very stature seemed to prevent fires. Every day he would walk through the town displaying that impressive uniform on his broad majestic figure; he would chat with people on the street and drop in on his friends. And even though he never even hinted at fire regulations, when a cigarette butt was smoldering somewhere, two or three people would vie with one another to see who could step on it first. During his fourteen years of service there had not been one fire in the town.

His reputation and the general esteem surrounding him was not merely the result of his expertise as a fire fighter. Neither were his functions in the village restricted to fire prevention: at weddings he sat at the head table; when wills were contested, he was the final judge; in political debates, his was the last word; when a fireplace needed rebuilding he was the first to be consulted; and when someone died, the coroner was summoned only after Toth had pronounced the irrevocable sentence: "The poor soul—he's gone to meet his maker."

Toth didn't know a whit more than anyone else about fireplaces or legal matters or smoking ham for that matter. He always advised precisely what others did but always seemed to utter his verdict one minute earlier than anyone else. And since most people did not realize that what Toth said could have occurred to them as well, the fire chief had gradually emerged as one of the smartest men around. Whatever he did was done well. Whenever he kicked a stone, it always stopped at the right, the only possible resting place; no matter what that place was, it became the stone's predestined location. A reputation is like a seal on a legal document: it has nothing to do with the meaning of the document, yet confers credibility on it.

Anyone in Toth's position would have thought twice before walking down Main Street with his helmet pulled over his eyes. But Toth yielded to Mariska's imploring glances because her face seemed to reflect the face of his beloved son. So the fire chief stoutly pulled down his helmet.

"All right," he grumbled. "Here I am, looking like a fool! Is there anything else you want?"

"Nothing, dearest. You're so wonderful, dear Lajos."

"You look great, Papa," Agi chimed in. "In fact you look a lot better this way. You're so handsome!"

"What a wonderful solution! It never would have occurred to me!" the major admitted appreciatively.

Toth registered these compliments with a somber air; his face did not light up even when they all started their procession home. Had he not been forced to pull his helmet down, Toth would have noticed that their homecoming was almost like a victory parade. Wherever they passed, windows opened, curtains fluttered, shadows flickered. The Szabos carried their paralyzed grandfather out to the front yard. Giza, the town's woman of ill-repute, hastily collected her drying underwear from the laundry line; carriages stopped on the road; children abandoned their games and stared at the quartet with open mouths.

The honored guest himself noticed none of this unusual interest. His mind was occupied with other things. First he peeked into the cisterns decorating the front lawns. Then his attention was diverted by a piece of string that lay coiled on the cement pavement and disappeared among the weeds on the side of the road. He carefully avoided stepping on it and warned Toth, "Careful, man! Don't step on it. It's a mine!" Further along they passed a Boy Scout troop coming in the opposite direction. Suddenly their leader blew his whistle and the major jumped behind a tree.

"How dare they make that noise!" he said angrily. But later, as they continued on their way, he said, "Sorry, I keep forgetting I'm at home."

When he had gotten off the bus he was already dead tired, and the long walk and additional excitement had exhausted him even more. By the time they reached the Toths' house, he could hardly stand.

The blooming hollyhocks didn't impress him, nor did the superb view from the porch. He didn't even notice the pine odor that permeated the house. Without any resistance, he let his host and hostess undress him, put a pair of pajamas on him, and lead him to bed. As soon as he lay down, he fell into a deep sleep and did not wake up until sundown.

As his eyelids were drooping on the threshold of sleep, he muttered something to Mariska that sounded like, "Dear Mariska, if an old hag dressed as a priest comes to the house and tries to exchange honeycomb for salt, shoot her in the head, please!"

"Just as you say, Major, sir," said Mrs. Toth to soothe him. She tiptoed out to the porch, where she sighed, with tears in her eyes, "The poor dear!"

"How much he must have suffered!" added little Agi through stifled sobs.

Only Toth stood there morosely without a trace of sympathy. A feeling of uncertainty was beginning to take hold of him.

"I would like to know what bothers him about me," he muttered.

"Lajos, dear, you do love to make mountains out of mole-hills."

"What do you mean? I can't even turn my head without making him jump. It's ridiculous!" Toth lamented.

"Don't worry, love. He'll come around. Let him have a good sleep; give him a chance to pull himself together! Just wait and see what happens then. After all, everybody loves you." Mariska's encouraging words had little effect.

Toth slowly shook his head. The future, he thought, boded ill. And at that very instant, as if echoing his doubts, Hektor, Professor Cipriani's prize-winning German shepherd, started howling menacingly.

CHAPTER TWO

Major Varro slept till late afternoon.

Mariska and Agi were scurrying about—cooking, baking, sewing, and washing—while the master of the house received callers. Many who had missed the triumphant march at noon crowded in to catch a glimpse of the esteemed visitor. Toth propelled them quietly, on tiptoe, to the major's bedroom, where the door had been left ajar.

"Come on, take a look," he whispered to the curious group.

He did not rush them. Anyone could stare at the sleeping major as long as he wished. Among the visitors were the schoolteacher, Miss Bakos, the local pastor, Father Tomaji, Sandor Soskuty, the engineer, and many other leading citizens. The last of them was Lorinc, a railroadman and Toth's next door neighbor. Everyone thought they were close friends because they'd worked on the railroad together, but, in reality, Lorinc was jealous of Toth.

Some years ago he had been injured as the result of a faulty train shunting, and his unpleasant personality had gotten worse after his accident. For months his whole upper torso, except his left arm, had been in a cast, and, after it was removed, an irritating itch remained. Beware the fury of a man with an itch! When the major arrived, Lorinc caused quite a stir by ostentatiously pulling down all the shades in his house. But now he not only put in an appearance, he even brought along a bottle of Mountain Rose Wine. He hoped to find the major awake, thinking they might sit down and drink some wine together and gradually become friends. Then, maybe he could lure the distinguished man away from Toth to his own house. But he was no luckier than the others. He got no farther than the door of the major's bedroom where he stopped and gaped. Frankly, there wasn't much to see. From where he stood there was nothing visible other than the bare sole of the major's right foot sticking out from under the blanket. Still, he was overwhelmed.

"What a nice tiny foot he has!" he remarked.

"It's a perfectly normal foot," Toth retorted, growing suspicious.

"I'm not saying it's not normal!" whispered his envious neighbor.

"It certainly sounded that way."

"Well, I didn't mean it that way," Lorinc protested. He was the kind who couldn't hide his nasty nature very well. "I was a bit surprised that's all. I never knew a human foot could look like that."

"Like what?"

"Forget it! I never said a word!" he said, beating a fast retreat. "His feet are perfectly normal."

"Stop this nonsense! Let me tell you Lorinc, every major has feet like that." Toth went on berating his neighbor as he pushed him out the door.

But the bad seed had been sown. Later Toth returned to the room, peered in, and examined his guest's foot with deep concentration. He viewed it as if it had been an independent entity and not part of a human body. But a part of what, then? Maybe it belonged to a lizard or some other cold-blooded creature or perhaps a species he had never encountered! Quickly he closed the door, hurried away, and lay down on his lounge chair where he soon fell asleep.

By the time Major Varro woke up, Mariska had washed and dried his uniform, shined all the brass buttons, and polished the stars on the lapel. Agi had cleaned his boots as much as was possible, rubbing them with a soft rag and spitting on them as lovingly as a mare licking her first foal. This labor of love took hours but, when the major finally reappeared in the family's company, the cracked and weather-beaten leather boots shone radiantly.

He looked gloomy.

"When you make sausage after you slaughter a pig, do you grind up the meat?" he asked.

"Yes," replied the Toths in unison.

"I dreamt that the partisans had kidnapped me and were grinding me up in a meat grinder—I could feel my bones cracking in its teeth."

"Good Lord!" exclaimed Mariska, horrified. "Did they smoke you after the grinding?"

"No, that was the extent of it," said the major. "Otherwise, I slept peacefully."

He looked well rested: not only did the uniform look more appealing, but its wearer did, too. The haunted expression had disappeared from his eyes and his voice sounded fresh and resonant. With gusto he devoured the chicken soup, the fried chicken, and the stewed fruit. After dinner he was in excellent spirits and asked to see the house and grounds.

The Toths were delighted when he finally admired the forest-covered Mt. Babony and its breathtaking view of the green valley. He noticed everything and praised the meticulous housekeeping and the well-kept garden. The all-pervading pine scent, in fact, almost moved him to tears.

"Dear friends," he announced as he returned to the glassed-in porch, "I am so glad I accepted your invitation. After nine months of constant stench and unbearable noise at the front I can't tell you how refreshed I feel."

Toasting the health of Gyula Toth, he raised his glass and gulped down the wine to the last drop. Now it was time for his hosts to feel moved. "And how glad we were when you so graciously accepted our invitation to spend your leave in our humble home," stuttered Mariska in a voice choking with emotion. "And *we* couldn't have dreamed of a better commander for our beloved son."

"As far as Gyula is concerned, you don't have to worry about him anymore," declared the major. "When the cold weather sets in I will personally have him transferred to a well-heated barracks reserved for officers; it's behind the lines, you know. Not only will he be out of the cold; his life will be out of danger."

Then he gave them a friendly nod and went off to his room. The Toth family was silent; the overpowering gratitude almost suffocated them. All the excitement of these past weeks, all the trouble, the extra work, and endless concern for Gyula had now been rewarded. The small bud of hope had burst into blossom and might even bear fruit!

"You see, Lajos my sweet," sighed Mariska, "a little bit of good will can produce miracles!"

Darkness had fallen. Mariska pulled Agi and her husband up close and they spent a few happy moments together in domestic serenity. Above them glimmered the star-dusted late July sky. The mountain, like a giant green lung exhaled its evening breeze over them. From the bedroom they could hear the slow, calm steps of the major. The Toths were delighted to have him so near, right in their own house. "Isn't it lovely," thought Mariska. "He had two helpings of the fried chicken, and he enjoyed the rich pine smell. . . . Gyula, Gyula! We pray to God that you reap the fruits of this visit! We hope the officers' quarters will really be heated! We hope the partisans don't venture too near! Gyula, Gyula! Don't let yourself get hurt. Don't let yourself freeze to death!"

For fifteen minutes they sat together in deep silence. They took it for granted that their distinguished guest had fallen asleep by now. They, too, were utterly exhausted by the day's activities.

Mariska had started for the bedroom when Toth decided to have a quick cigar. He inhaled with sensuous pleasure. He loved the small joys of life: the cool breeze, the comfort of his armchair, the closeness of his loved ones, the rich aroma of his cigar. When these little pleasures could be enjoyed all at once, he would stretch and moan and turn his thoughts to his mother.

Now, pulling himself up a bit, he gave his joints a good

crack and emitted a low wholesome groan: "Oh, Mother, Mother, dear old Mother, why have you left me?"

It was the last time Toth stretched and moaned for the next two weeks, for at that instant the door flew open and in rushed the major looking alarmed.

"What is the matter? Has someone been wounded?" he yelled.

"Nothing is the matter," responded the slightly embarrassed fire chief, trying to calm his guest.

"But I heard someone moan."

"It was me, sir."

With a bashful smile Toth explained that stretching was an old habit and whenever he stretched, he moaned and groaned along with it. There was nothing to worry about: he only did this when he was feeling tip top.

"I'm delighted to hear that," said the major curtly.

He gave Toth a long look and returned to his room. The family was stunned and had no idea how to react. But they didn't have long to think because their guest soon reappeared. He circled his host twice and said, "Well, what's new, Toth?"

"Nothing at all, sir."

"Still feeling fine?"

"Nothing to complain about, sir."

"And what makes you feel so good?"

"What? Hmmm. I don't know. I just do."

The major examined Toth like a specimen, which made him feel rather self-conscious. He drew only short puffs from his cigar until the major finally went back to his room. But before long the major stormed in again, and again inspected Toth.

"Has anything happened?"

"No, not a thing."

"But your cigar is no longer burning."

"That's true," confessed the fire chief. "I snubbed it out."

"What are you doing on the porch anyway?"

"Just enjoying the fresh air."

"Nothing else?"

"Well, not really," admitted Toth after a few seconds'

thought. Toth could not tell if this explanation satisfied the major or not. What he could tell though was that after this last exchange the major took much less time in returning to the porch than before.

"Tell me, Toth," he confronted the now trembling man, "would you like to play a game of chess with me?"

"I'm sorry, major, I don't play chess."

"Would you rather play cards?"

"Sorry, I don't know a single card game," apologized Toth.

"What about dominoes?"

Toth hardly dared breathe as he stuttered his reply. "The fact is, sir, the fact is, I don't know any games at all."

The major could hardly conceal his disapproval as he spun sharply and returned to his room. They couldn't even hear his steps. Not a sound filtered through the walls. It was terribly depressing. They sat motionless, avoiding one another's eyes, as if mesmerized by the sudden silence from within.

This time it was several long minutes before the door was thrown open again. Toth tried to back up while still sitting in his chair, but the major headed straight for him, leaned over, and fixed him with a piercing glare.

"My dear Toth," he said, "I hope I'm not embarrassing you!"

"Not at all."

"Then let's talk openly. Aren't you missing something?"

"Only my cherrywood cigarette holder, but it's hardly worth mentioning. Anyway, I can always carve another."

"I don't mean material things. I was trying to make you see the dangerous consequences of idleness, the dire effects of sloth."

Toth was utterly confused. He looked in vain to his wife for help, but she, in turn, was waiting for him to unscramble what the major had said.

"I see you don't understand." Major Varro assumed a lecturing position. "Listen, my dear Toth family! In a dark room even the softest noise sounds amplified—the volume is multiplied a hundred times. Now idleness has the same effect on the entire human organism as darkness on the organs of hearing: it reinforces internal sounds, causes distorted vision, and creates a rattling in the brain. Whenever my soldiers have nothing to do, I order them to cut off all their trouser buttons. Then they have to sew them back on. As a result, they are always calm and collected. Now do you see my point?"

The Toths stared at one another, more confused than ever.

"But sir," ventured Mariska after some hesitating, "if your trouser buttons have come undone, I will be more than happy to sew them back."

"You don't see my point at all," said the major waving impatiently. "At least, tell me whether you have a badly tangled ball of string around the house."

"We can certainly find some," the lady of the house lighted up. "And what do you need it for, sir?"

"To untangle it!" replied the guest nervously. "I can't sit around all day as idly as you."

"But why didn't you say so?" Agi interjected in her melodious voice. It was not the first time she had grasped the situation more quickly than her elders. "Mother and I never sit with our hands in our laps; we always have something to do."

"And what do you do?"

"Every night about this time, when there are no chores to do, we usually make boxes."

The major's eyes lit up. "Boxes you say?" he exclaimed. "Very interesting! What kind of boxes?"

With the war, production at the Eger Bandage Works had skyrocketed. Since the factory had only one boxing machine, large supplies of cotton, gauze, and first-aid kits backed up and lay unpacked for weeks. To ease the situation the company had taken on some extra help, even half-Jews. The work could easily be done at home. The local people gladly participated in this enterprise, not only because it made them feel as if they were contributing to the war effort, but also because it meant a little extra money.

The Toths received thousands of pieces of cardboard. Mariska would cut along the dotted lines; Agi would fold them. As for the master of the house, he just sat watching the womenfolk tenderly, sometimes smiling at their diligence while he puffed on his cigar. When it got late, he would often doze off, and then Mariska worked extra carefully so as not to wake him with the noise of the cutting. Her paper cutter looked almost like a professional piece of equipment. Mr. Toth had made it himself from a few discarded boards and an old kitchen knife. With this masterpiece Mariska could cut the required shapes from the cardboard more easily than with ordinary scissors.

It had never occurred to anyone that Toth might also take part in this activity. The dignity of a District Fire Chief would not permit him to demean himself with such a menial task so obviously designed for the delicate hands of a woman.

Major Varro was less particular about his dignity.

He examined the huge crispy sheets of cardboard with visible delight and watched excitedly as the paper cutter was screwed to the table. As soon as the folding began, he became totally engrossed in the work. He pulled his chair near the cutter to get a better look at it. Despite the courteous protests of his hosts he immediately began folding boxes with precision. After a few practice moves, he was adept at handling the cutter as well.

"Goodness me! What skillful hands he has!" marveled Mariska.

"He does twice as many as the two of us together!" exclaimed Agi.

Did the major hear them? If so, he never let on: his eyelids didn't flicker and his hands kept moving with a steady rhythm. He didn't stop for a second. They all worked like machines without uttering a sound. When they had finished a large pile of boxes, the major looked up and turned to Toth. "How about you? Won't you join us?" he inquired.

"Me?" Toth seemed dumbfounded at first, but then laughed heartily. The women, too, smiled at this absurd suggestion. But the major did not smile. Instead, he urged the fire chief to fold at least one box. Toth gave in and produced an un-box-like mass which immediately collapsed in his lap.

"No, really, this is not for me," he protested.

"Why not?"

"I'm no good with my hands."

"Neither am I! You don't need to be to put this simple thing together!"

People often (for example, when excited) say things they don't mean. Toth, however, was perfectly calm. He could have sworn he had given the major a respectful, indeed, almost humble, reply, something along the lines of, "The major is really bucked up by this activity."

But these unassuming words conveyed themselves to the major as, "The major is really fucked up in this activity."

At first Major Varro stared at Toth, then he turned pale. His eyes narrowed, and the box fell out of his hand as he jumped up quivering with emotion. "I demand you repeat what you have just said!" he bellowed.

"I said, 'The major is really bucked up by this.' "

"Did you hear that?" the major asked the women. His face had turned a bright crimson, and veins stood out at his temples. His voice trembled with uncontrollable indignation. "By what right do you dare talk to me in this manner? I am a major in the Hungarian Army. At the front the punishment for such an insult to an officer is instant death."

Dead silence. An indescribable silence, the kind that one finds in a mass grave where only deaf and dumb people are buried. No one had the courage to break it. Any comment might further complicate an already complicated situation.

For the major was not the only insulted party here. Toth was equally wounded, and rightly so. He was thoroughly convinced he had said nothing wrong. And having one's good intentions misconstrued is a humiliation of the worst order.

Even Mariska seemed disturbed. She had clearly heard him say "bucked," and a devoted wife who loves and respects her spouse always hears what he says. Of course, she respected and loved the major too. What could she do? Looking like a frightened bird, she sat there frozen, blinking first at Toth, then at the major.

What about Agi? As if in a trance, she peered over at her father, her rosy face growing darker and darker. She had heard neither "bucked" nor "fucked." She had heard "sucked." Something had gone terribly wrong here.

Nature inoculates children with a serum that makes them sensitive to their fathers' shortcomings. Agi represented the one case in a thousand that had been spared. Although she had distinctly heard her father say "sucked," she decided not to believe her ears rather than assume that her father could stoop so low. She therefore screwed up her courage, stood up, and screamed in a high-pitched voice, "How *can* you insinuate that a vulgar word like that could ever leave my father's lips!"

"Agi's right!" shouted Mariska in agreement. "It must have been a misunderstanding. My husband never insulted anyone! Isn't that right, dear?"

"Never!" said Toth, who had been clearly shaken by the incident. "Once I happened to mistake Professor Cipriani's wife for a scarecrow and rudely turned my back on her. But that was just a silly accident. I would never be able to insult the honorable major. Not even by mistake."

The major faltered. "Perhaps I misunderstood you," he muttered, "But I do not wish for such a misunderstanding to occur again."

The Toths relaxed. They swore it would never ever happen again. The major was pacified.

"Let's forget the whole thing, Toth," he said magnanimously. "Let's go back to the boxes. Every moment counts."

They all settled down to work, Toth included. The selfsame Toth who had had nothing but contempt for box-making, who had considered it women's work, was now delighted to participate. The others were almost reluctant to let him squeeze in with his chair. And though, try as he might, he could produce only misshapen boxes with his huge, clumsy hands, his coworkers merely smiled indulgently and refrained from comment.

Peace had been restored. For some time no one spoke; the only sound was the banging of the paper cutter.

A fresh breeze from the mountain blew over them; small bonfires, marking the camps of sap gatherers, glowed along the slopes of Mt. Babony. The Toths did not notice them.

They were oblivious to everything in the outside world; their entire world was cutting and shaping boxes.

After a good hour the major asked, "Is anyone getting tired?"

Toth, who was barely able to keep his eyes open, assured the major he had no intention of going to bed yet.

So the work went on and on. Some time later when the major solicitously repeated his question, they unanimously declared they were not sleepy.

When he asked a third time, Mariska, whose left eye had begun to itch rather painfully, answered that if the major wished to rest, they, too, would be willing to stop.

"Me? Rest? Not at all!" said the major. "I have insomnia and I can't sleep too well."

"The clear biting mountain air has always soothed the nerves of our previous guests suffering from insomnia," commented Toth.

"I'm beyond helping," insisted the major. "I can probably fold boxes until morning."

The box in Toth's hands suddenly crumpled into a heap. Accustomed to retiring early, his features were by now ravished by fatigue. He stared in terror at the major. But when Mariska kicked him gently he managed to feign a smile and murmur, "Good. I'm just beginning to get the hang of it."

So on they went.

Postcard from the front:

My Dear Parents and Agi,

Here we are in Kursk. I am writing this in a hurry because we are going to the public baths and then must rush back. There is one thing I forgot to tell you about the major: you must find some activity for him in the evenings. His strained nerves have given him insomnia, and he sleeps during the day. At sundown, when the danger of partisan attack is greatest, he craves company. We usually play cards with him or make up different games to divert his attention and alleviate his boredom. He doesn't like anyone to go to bed; in fact, the slightest indication of sleepiness upsets him terribly. Please think of my plight and try to accommodate him.   (Delayed)

At 1:15 A.M. Lajos Toth yawned. He had often yawned before. This simple manifestation of exhaustion had never had any particular consequence. This time, however, he was aware of a strange stillness that followed his yawning. Of course, it had been quiet before, but at this moment the silence made him feel as if he were enveloped by a strange, cold air bubble. All of them looked at him. He, too, would have liked to see his own face but that wasn't possible.

At last the major, who was holding the paper cutter, asked, "What's the matter?"

"I yawned," confessed Toth.

Another silence followed. Everybody gazed at him again. No one said he was not supposed to yawn, but Toth had gathered as much by now. Gradually he realized he had committed a grave error.

"It's my fault," said the major, looking more sad than insulted. "I shouldn't have taken it for granted that you enjoyed a bit of healthy work as much as I do."

"But I'm not really sleepy," protested Toth.

"Then why did you yawn?"

"Oh, when I yawn, it doesn't mean that I'm tired," answered Toth lying through his teeth.

"Are you trying to say that you are still feeling fine?" asked the major sarcastically. "You mean you yawn to show how fit you feel?"

"That's right," said Toth.

"That's the way he is," said Mariska with forced brightness.

"Yes, that's how Papa is," agreed Agi.

It was not easy to convince the major.

"Tell me honestly, what would you like to do most: fold boxes or go to bed?" he asked Toth.

"Oh! Fold boxes!" declared the fire chief enthusiastically in a tone that excluded any further argument.

"Well, if you insist, we may as well continue," conceded the guest.

So they went on cutting and folding. Gradually the stars began to lose their glow; on the slopes of Mt. Babony the bonfires died down to smoldering embers. The sap gatherers had gone home in the morning light.

"It's getting late," admitted the major. "Are you sure you don't want to go to bed?"

"Oh, no," said Mariska.

"Not me," chirped Agi, fully alert.

Toth also protested, but since his tongue was no longer functioning, all that came out was a gurgling sound. The work went on.

There was no sign of fatigue about the major. Agi's hands moved rapidly too; girls her age can go on forever. Mariska was feeling numb all over; she couldn't feel her legs at all, though fortunately her hands still obeyed her. Toth was in terrible shape: his mind was muddled; he couldn't control his limbs; and he had started hallucinating. Once he nearly toppled over to make way for an express train that zoomed across the porch. The boxes he produced looked like lopsided dumplings.

A cock began to crow. Toth didn't hear it. Day was dawning; darkness was giving way to light. He didn't notice that either. Suddenly the major stopped working.

"The sun is rising. Time for bed," he said.

They all stood except Toth who mechanically crumpled up one more box.

"I can't tell you how pleasant it's been," the major declared.

"Oh, yes, we've enjoyed it, too," Mariska responded with a smile.

"I hope we can continue tomorrow."

"Of course we can," said Agi.

"Pleasant dreams," said the major departing.

"Good night," whispered Mariska, hardly able to enunciate the words.

After the major retired, the Toths lingered on. They were exhausted, too tired even to move. Toth's head hung over his lap; he couldn't even close his eyes—they had the glassy stare of a fish in a chowder pot. Suddenly his head fell on the table and he began to snore.

111

The women mustered up enough strength between them to get him to his feet. They dragged his giant body to the bedroom and with a great heave managed to get it on the bed. It landed with a heavy thud like a monumental column toppling over.

The sun was up.

CHAPTER THREE

The Toths had a handsome scrapbook bound in red leather; it was one of their most treasured possessions. They kept it primarily for the messages and impressions of their houseguests. Here are a few samples:

> Ever since the tragic departure of my beloved spouse, I had been afflicted by unbearable insomnia and lack of appetite. These symptoms ceased here as if I had been touched by a magic wand. Your mountain air has cured me completely.
>
> [Mrs. Gustav Morvai, Widow]

> This house is an island of tranquility where men who hate the hustle and bustle of modern life can at last find peace.
>
> [Aladar Filatori, Tympanist of the Opera]

> While the nation is waging a life and death struggle against the terror of the Red Bolsheviks, the butter rolls and meals served here have given me renewed strength to carry on the heroic fight.
>
> [Ferenc Kaszony, Compagnie Internationale
> des Wagons-Lits, Conductor)

> Röslein, Röslein, Röslein fein
> Röslein auf der Heide!
>
> [Karoly G. Hammermann, Pig Slaughterer]

After such an exhausting night Toth felt like sleeping all day, but life cannot come to a standstill, not even for a major. The chief had to write his fire report for headquarters, fetch water from the artesian well, inspect the district, chop wood for the pastor, and so forth. Agi had to go shopping and feed the chickens, and Mariska had innumerable chores. In addition to the care of her guest, she had to do the Ciprianis' wash and clean the pastor's house—to mention only a few of her responsibilities.

Moreover, the entire household had been turned topsy-turvy since the major arrived. Since he woke up in the afternoon, they ate breakfast at lunchtime; what they now called lunch they used to call dinner; and what they should have now called dinner, they didn't call anything, for when dinnertime came, they were all in bed.

That first morning, having had one and a half hours of sleep, Toth opened his eyes only after repeated calls and shakes. He was depressed and dead tired in body and soul; he languidly stared into space. Thinking through the last night and projecting into the future, he remarked with considerable annoyance, "I'm afraid all this will come to no good! Just wait and see, my dear Mariska!"

His loyal wife gave him a glass of warm milk and quietly placed the scrapbook on his lap. She reminded him of the state Mr. Hammermann had been in when he came to them. And the Morvai widow. And all the others! In this ideal environment they had all recovered rapidly. Had he forgotten Mr. Host, the aged painter charged with restoring the frescoes in the cupola of the basilica? The unusual spatial contrast between the cupola and the frescoes had disrupted his equilibrium to such an extent that the poor man had lost all sense of balance. When he arrived at the Toths', he was convinced the floor of their house was so steep that he couldn't cross the room without holding onto a piece of string stretched out between the two doorknobs. But the fresh mountain air had cured even him. His comment in the scrapbook read: "No strings attached! In excellent spirits, I depart from this enchanted place."

"Remember, dear Lajos, how frayed his nerves were?" recalled Mariska. "And he came to us from a church. Think of our major, who comes from the front! We must not lose heart. Even if it takes a bit longer, the major's balance will be restored. Watch—in no time he'll be healthy again!"

But Toth honestly did not believe such rapid improvement was possible for their guest. "What if we have to make boxes every night, all night long? A normal human being can't live without sleep, Mariska!"

His misgivings about box making every night proved correct, but he didn't realize how quickly human nature can adapt to new situations. Of course, eight hours of uninterrupted sleep is the ideal, but stealing ten minutes here, a quarter of an hour there, can be just as satisfactory. It soon became apparent that they could doze off while having groceries weighed or watering Cipriani's famous tulips or letting the soup cool or waiting for the coffee to perk. They could catch quick naps under the table while picking up fallen items. Even during the box-making sessions they did not have to kill themselves every minute.

To the Toths' profound joy, the major became so absorbed in the work that from the second night on he devoted his total attention to the paper cutter. Since he had to cut eight slits on each sheet of cardboard, he soon fell behind the Toths (who did only the folding and were, after all, three against one). But the major wouldn't capitulate: without a second's break he went on rapturously cutting. Still, despite his breakneck speed, the Toths remained way ahead and were eventually able to relax a bit.

At first they rested only their hands. Later they closed their eyes and breathed through their noses. They found this to be quite relaxing. But since the major was blind to the outside world, they gradually grew bolder: they hid a lounge chair behind some spruce trees in the garden and disappeared periodically, taking turns at this much deserved, if pilfered, rest.

"May I be excused," they would say—as if they were asking permission to relieve themselves—and then sneak out for a fifteen- or twenty-minute nap in the cool garden.

Meanwhile Major Varro was happily adjusting the cardboard under the knife, lifting the cutting arm, and slicing away, slicing away. He didn't even notice when on the third day the Toths started disappearing in pairs, because as soon as they returned they easily caught up with him. Still, he must have suspected something because once, when all three of them were working at the table (to be truthful, Toth was merely staring into space), he suddenly interrupted his cutting and asked in a strange tone, "What's going on here?"

"Nothing in particular," said Toth.

"Then what are you looking at?"

"Only a butterfly. It just flew in."

"What kind of butterfly?"

"I don't know. But it has yellow wings with three red dots," replied Toth.

"Why bother with such details now?" asked the guest.

"I just happened to see it," apologized the fire chief.

"Just happened to, eh?" repeated the major rather angrily. "I'll bet you were thinking of catching it and killing it."

Toth was shocked.

"How could you say such a thing, Major, sir?"

"It's true, isn't it? That's exactly what you were doing!"

"Well, it did occur to me just for a moment," admitted Toth.

"Just as I suspected!" shouted the major.

He started to pace the room casting annoyed glances at Toth, who sat there with downcast eyes, looking contrite even though he didn't have the slightest idea what crime he had committed. The major soon set him straight.

"Listen my friends," he said with suppressed indignation, "even though I am very grateful for your hospitality, we can't go on like this anymore. If you insist on thinking of other things while we are working, the whole point of our work is lost."

No one spoke. Toth knew he had made another error, but didn't know how to rectify it.

"I am in complete agreement with our honorable major," he remarked humbly, "but it is impossible for me to prevent thoughts from entering my head."

"Nonsense! A dog has four legs, yet it doesn't run in four directions at once. Or have you seen a dog running in four directions?"

After due reflection Toth was forced to confess that he had never seen such a dog yet.

"I hurt my own brother's feelings by declining to spend my

leave with his family. If you want me to stay, you had better make certain nothing like this ever happens again!"

Toth swore on everything holy—he was willing to make any sacrifice, but he did not quite know what the major expected of them.

"I have a feeling we don't understand each other too well," said the major, annoyed. "Let me give you an example. You eat regularly, don't you?"

Toth acquiesced and said that he usually did.

"Now what does it involve? Food intake, chewing, salivation, and swallowing. A complex, continuous, uninterrupted process. And to make my point perfectly clear, let me give you another example. Do you know our national anthem?" Toth nodded.

"Please sing the first line!"

"God bless the Hungarians!"

"Correct!" applauded the major. "Now, did you think of anything while you sang the words?"

Toth couldn't recall thinking of anything.

"There, that's precisely what I mean! Now do you see my point?"

Toth conceded that everything was a great deal clearer, but here and there a few vague spots remained.

"Then let's clarify them!" said the major.

This time he chose an example from army life. It was the major's experience that temporary idleness was always more harmful that complete inactivity: a person who did absolutely nothing could at least organize his thoughts, while a person who moved back and forth between activity and inactivity inevitably became the victim of idle thoughts during the transition from one state to the other. This was exactly what had happened just now with Toth and the butterfly.

"Do you understand now?" inquired the guest.

Agi said she did. Toth said he almost did. Mariska said nothing out loud but silently sighed, "Poor Gyula!"

"Let me simplify matters," said Major Varro with infinite patience. "Dear Toth, ignore all these theoretical analyses. Just chase away all stray thoughts and daydreams while you work!

117

I'm certain it won't be any special trouble. Or do you have other suggestions, perhaps?"

Toth gazed straight ahead, a broken man. Mariska turned away to hide the tears running down her cheeks. They could not respond; they could think of nothing to say as they sat panic-stricken. Only the youngest member of the family remained calm.

"It's really very simple," said Agi. "The paper cutter is too small, and the major can't keep up with us."

"Bravo!" he exclaimed. "Your daughter has a brilliant mind, Toth. Now that she has identified the problem, the solution should be child's play."

It was dawn again. The major wished them good night and went to bed. And though everyone thinks that firemen and railroadmen can sleep at any time, this morning Toth was unable to get even a wink of sleep. He got up feeling wretched and continued to feel wretched all day. His head ached as he brooded and fretted. Anxiously he tried to think standing, sitting, even on a diagonal—all to no avail. When the major awoke and looked at Toth expectantly, he could only report, "I'm terribly sorry, sir, but so far I haven't come up with a thing."

"Don't worry about it," said the major by way of encouragement. "All good things come to those who wait."

This pacified poor Toth to some extent, and they all sat down to breakfast (formerly lunch). Mariska had soothed her nerves by baking a sponge cake. At the conclusion of the meal Toth stood up unexpectedly and declared in a trembling voice, "I think I have it, sir!"

"Congratulations!" rejoiced the guest. "Tell us!"

Toth frowned and looked perturbed as he sat down. "It's gone. I've lost it."

The major showed no sign of impatience; indeed, he was almost tender. He called for complete silence and ordered strong coffee and a cigar. Toth drank down the coffee and lit up the cigar. Fifteen minutes passed. Suddenly Toth cried out, "It's coming. . . . It's coming. . . . It's beginning to take shape. . . ."

"I knew it!" cried the major happily patting Toth on the shoulder.

The major had never before touched anyone in the house, and Toth was so taken aback that the minute he felt the major's hand on his shoulder, the idea abandoned him. But the major didn't mind that either. By now he was treating Toth as a mother treats her child. He even made up endearing nicknames for him. But it didn't seem to help; in fact, the more cordial the major became, the more depressed Toth felt.

Although his mind kept pounding like a sledgehammer, the only results were the following:

At 4:10 he said nothing was forthcoming.

At 4:20 still nothing.

At 4:35 he reported that something important was shaping up in his brain.

Seven minutes later he stood up and said he thought he was on the right track, but didn't want to rush into any premature conclusions.

At 4:45 he announced, "I've got it!"

His face was flushed, his eyes glowing.

"Major Varro, sir," he announced at five after five, "I've just had a daring idea: since the old paper cutter is too small, what we need is a bigger one." And thoroughly exhausted after this revelation, he collapsed in an armchair.

The major gave his sincere thanks and expressed his heartfelt admiration for Toth in a few choice words of praise.

Toth thanked him with a tired smile.

Major Varro politely inquired whether this most promising venture could be accomplished without too much trouble.

Toth assured him that it was really quite easy. Since he'd already built a smaller cutter, he'd certainly be able to construct a larger one.

Next question: would the new machine cut more pieces of cardboard?

Answer: as many as five sheets at once.

Then the major ventured to ask "my Lajos" (by now his terms of endearment were positively unctuous) when it might be convenient for him to begin preparing the new cutter.

Right away, if necessary. The raw material was ready. Toth already had a board that could serve as the base; all that was needed was an iron bar to hone into a cutting blade.

"Well, let's get on with it then!" shouted the major with enthusiasm. "Every moment counts!"

Theoretically speaking, a timepiece will tell time more or less accurately forever, provided, of course, it doesn't break down or wear out.

Take, for instance, Toth's watch, an old-fashioned pocketwatch from his railroad days. What do you think would happen if Toth's watch were squeezed to half of its original size (in such a way that nothing was damaged)? Of course, the watch would be half its original size, but wouldn't the time it told be only half the original time? The human mind can be compared to such a watch: violent interference may alter its primary functions drastically. The only function of a watch is to tell time; the function of the human mind is considerably more complex. Its function is to register: it receives, sorts out, and stores various sensory impressions from the outside world. It also remembers: it can look into the past as well as into the future and is capable of concrete and abstract deductions. Even more amazing is its ability to name objects: it calls a chicken a chicken. It can also construct a cupola on top of a cathedral in Florence and possesses the knowledge (conscious or unconscious) that tells us to eat meat grilled on glowing embers rather than the embers themselves. Indeed, its functions are countless.

Though not the type to set the world on fire, Toth had thus far managed to carry out all the basic functions of human existence. He would doubtless have continued to do so had it not been for the violent interference from without, which, metaphorically speaking, had reduced his intellectual functions by half.

But can we honestly label Major Varro's two weeks' stay a violent interference? Yes, in Toth's case this assessment seems justified.

Fire fighting is a highly complex task, and Toth had always

lived in a perpetual state of readiness. As soon as he noticed a wisp of smoke, his brain immediately signalled him that the Kasztriners were burning leaves. It would signal him with the same accuracy if that smoke heralded a devastating fire.

In such a case, however, his brain would trigger a much more complex response: he would jump out of bed, sound the alarm, drive the firetruck to the scene, and pump water on the source of the flames. That this had never happened is quite irrelevant. A man is worth not only what he is, but what he is capable of being as well.

In addition to being a superb fireman, Toth had several other admirable qualities which further enhanced his solidly rounded reputation. For instance, he had once dismantled the Ciprianis' waterpump, oiled it, and put it back together again. He had fixed chairs with rickety legs with the masterly hammering of one nail into the right place. When his family began making boxes for the Eger Bandage Works, it was he who had skillfully designed and constructed the homemade paper cutter from an old kitchen knife. And this gadget had been working perfectly ever since. But now that he was called upon to make a bigger machine out of a smaller one rather than something out of nothing, all that his mind could squeeze out were a few childish ideas, and even that little he could produce only with superhuman effort.

The theory that anxiety and fear are detrimental to proper functioning of the brain cells is borne out by the case of Lajos Toth. In order to comprehend the forthcoming events, it is of paramount importance to recall a previous statement, for when not long beforehand Toth had sighed and declared, "I'm afraid all this will come to no good," he had in fact foreseen his unhappy destiny with uncanny clarity.

What followed was all the more peculiar because no sooner did Toth present his guest with the new paper cutter than their run-ins ceased, and the major replaced his endless nit-picking with loyal, charming friendliness. For a while Toth seemed to have regained his equilibrium. Then, one glorious summer morning, on the eighth day of the major's visit and three days after the celebrated installation of the new machine, for no apparent reason and with the irresponsibility of an adolescent, Lajos Toth ran away from home at exactly 3:06 A.M.

They searched desperately for him everywhere, but to no avail. Finally, late the next afternoon Father Tomaji spotted the fire chief cowering under his giant bed.

It would be unfair to lay the blame entirely on Major Varro for this inexplicable move. It should be noted, however, that just before this unusual behavior, a few insignificant incidents did occur, and each therefore must be told, even though they seem to throw an unfavorable light on our Mr. Toth.

After almost two days of hard labor, the new paper cutter was completed.

This contraption was so heavy that Toth staggered under its weight as he lugged it up from the basement. It was as wide as a full-grown man and its blade, which went through cardboard like a knife through butter, could cut a calf in two; its cutting arm looked like a medieval executioner's axe and had the thud of a meat cleaver.

They all walked around it, gaping in total amazement. The major was thrilled, almost ecstatic: he fingered, patted, and punched his new toy, itching to see it in action. The women slid in three, four, five sheets of cardboard at once and the gadget worked like a dream; it cut evenly without any trouble. Its efficiency surpassed all expectations.

After casting one last admiring glance at the miraculous machine, the major walked over to Toth and solemnly announced, "I really don't know how to express my gratitude, dear Toth, but this much I will tell you: until now I have shared my quarters with Lt. Hellebrandt, but as soon as I get back to the front, your son will take his place. I live in a school building surrounded by a double guard, and my quarters, of course, are a great deal safer than the army barracks. No, please don't thank me. We don't want to waste valuable time on mundane matters. Now let's have dinner and then off to work!"

They sat down to eat. It was the most memorable dinner in Mariska's life. Not only was she finally certain her son would be safe, she was also happy that the major was so demonstrative in his appreciation of her husband's talent. Varro kept smiling at Toth and insisted that all the best pieces of chicken liver be given to him. He winked at Mariska mischievously as adults do when exchanging glances over an act that would definitely spoil the child.

At last lunch (formerly dinner) ended. There were still kitchen chores to attend to: the two women had to clean off the table, wash the dishes, and finally carry in the cardboard. The major, however, was impatient, finding even this brief pause too much to bear. He turned to Toth and said, "What do you say we have a beer, Toth my boy?"

It was a sign of how far their relationship had progressed that the major called Toth "Toth my boy" when the fire chief, even without his helmet, was a good deal taller than he.

The two men walked over to Klein's Beer Garden and settled at a table on the patio. At first they had only a beer, then beer laced with rum, and before long they switched to straight rum.

The major became more and more talkative. He began to lose his military inhibitions and confessed that he was having a marvelous time with the Toths, in fact, he was having the time of his life.

Toth thanked him graciously.

Later, the major explained that his feeling of well-being was due primarily to the healthy, relaxing activity of making boxes. Every day he woke up anticipating the evening's work with such impatience that he could hardly wait until they started.

Toth nodded sympathetically.

There was something indefinably majestic and noble in this pursuit. Such collective labor was far superior to playing cards, more entertaining and challenging than chess. Making boxes was the best thing in the world!

Toth agreed wholeheartedly.

"How good it would be," the major said dreamily, if more and more people could join box-making groups. Perhaps the time will come when the entire population, better yet, all mankind will pursue this rewarding task."

"Yes," Toth acquiesced. "It would be extremely productive."

"Each nation could produce boxes of a different color and shape. The name might vary, but in the final analysis a box is a box, right?"

"Undoubtedly," replied Toth promptly.

"At that time the entire human race would bless our names for introducing them to box making," the major went on.

"Oh, my Lord, my Lord," Toth moaned absentmindedly.

Major Varro gazed into the distance and said no more. Men usually hide their emotions, but the major's eyes betrayed him. He was in a state of exaltation, exhilaration; a wild dream was about to come true. . . . He paid for the drinks without a word and, as if under a spell, took Toth by the arm. They marched home like old friends.

Mariska greeted them at the garden gate.

From time immemorial, women have been restless when their men go out for beer. Although she had no idea when their spree would end, she had stood waiting anxiously and watching the street with stoic perseverance. Now she could hardly believe her eyes. As her loved ones got closer, the two figures seemed to blend into one; their figures blurred and gradually faded into the shape of Gyula, her son. Lithe and elegant in his medal-studded uniform, happy and smiling, without a scratch, he was waving a huge salami. The dear boy never came home empty-handed. . . . Oh Gyula!

Postcard from the front:

Dear Mr. and Mrs. Toth and Family,

I drove the car that took Major Varro to the Kursk railroad station. On our way home, your son and I went to the public baths. Then we had a couple of beers. We started rather early, but even so, it got dark on our way back. What actually happened later, I can only guess at. Nobody could have thrown a hand grenade at us because both sides of the highway were cleared of trees for about a hundred meters on either side. And it was too dark for anybody to shoot at us. The last thing I remember is a cloud of pink smoke rising from the car's motor. Although I suffered only minor injuries, mainly from glass fragments from the windshield, I was totally unconscious at first. Later I managed to crawl as far as the next village to get help. By the time we got back to what remained of the car, our beloved Ensign Toth was gone. Perhaps he was unharmed and walked away under his own power. It is equally possible that he was wounded and picked up by a German armored car. Had I not been so dizzy and in shock, I would be able to give you a more accurate account. All I can say is that I hope that my friend, the ensign, has escaped without injury.

Respectfully,
Sandor Gyurica, enlisted driver.

(Needless to say the postcard met a watery fate in the rain barrel.)

The one-meter-long cutting arm of the new paper cutter slammed down with a thud, jerking the Toths into motion. They were happy, smiling, full of enthusiasm. One could scarcely imagine a more idyllic picture. First the major slid three . . . four . . . then five sheets of cardboard under the blade. The gadget functioned flawlessly. Such success made the major almost drunk with joy. He began flooding the room with cut pieces, shouting, "More, more! Faster! Let's go!"

There was no more time for resting, catnapping or daydreaming, they all worked without let up until dawn. But it didn't matter to them as long as they knew their darling Gyula would be safe from now on.

As Mariska observed when they staggered back to their rooms, utterly exhausted, "You see, my sweet Lajos, just a bit of good will can work miracles!"

Toth, no longer able to speak, gave an assenting grunt. Even in his total prostration, he seemed peaceful, almost happy. But how long would this peace last?

Two days.

The first sign of trouble came the night before Toth ran away, right after lunch (formerly dinner).

By the time the meal was over, the major had grown so impatient and restless that the whole house felt like an electric generating station. It had become his habit to take a walk with Toth while the ladies cleaned up and got ready. These strolls covered the road to the bus station three or four times, back and forth. That crucial night they set out eagerly to take a bit of fresh air. Who would have thought that an innocent walk would bring about such total calamity?

Matraszentanna has no streetlights, and when our men started their sauntering, it was dusk; the road was illuminated only by the stars of the August sky. This mysterious semidarkness was interrupted only by an occasional lit window.

It so happened that one of the windows belonged to Madame Giza, the local woman of ill-repute, whose house always shone at night, the better to steer her ardent customers in the right direction. If her bedroom window was dark, the next guest knew enough to wait: someone else had merely slipped in ahead of him. It was exactly this harmless routine that started the trouble.

In front of Madame Giza's window stood an electric transformer. Its squat iron box threw a slanted shadow across the road. During their walk to the bus station and back, Major Varro mistook the shadow for a ditch.

He stopped to gauge its width, took a running start, and leaped over it with great dexterity.

What else could Toth do? He also stopped, ran, and jumped. Had he acted otherwise, he would have embarrassed the major.

On they went. Back they came. And again they jumped over the transformer's shadow. This ritual was repeated several times as they went on breathing the fresh mountain air, chatting casually about nothing in particular.

Medical experts agree that people living at high altitudes are more active sexually than people living in the flatlands. It's no wonder, therefore, that Madame Giza's window turned dark again that night. When the two men returned to the house on their second round trip, there was no ditch in sight, nothing but an intact stretch of gray road. However, they stopped mechanically as before.

"After you," commanded the major examining the road.

"Only after you, sir!" replied Toth staring at the same spot.

"Out of question!" argued the guest. "I don't particularly care for polite games. Go!"

It was time to act. Lajos Toth had two alternatives.

1. Not to jump. That would indicate that the previous three times he had taken the major for a fool, because as a resident of the town he should have been well acquainted with its roads.

2. To jump. But that would make the major think he still saw a ditch where there had only been a shadow.

Of these equally outrageous, idiotic alternatives, Toth chose the lesser of two evils and, taking a running start, leaped once more over the nonexistent ditch.

It was now the major's turn. He, too, had two alternatives:

1. Not to jump, this would be tantamount to admitting that he had allowed a simpleminded municipal fireman to make a fool of him.

2. To jump, thereby showing that *he* still considered the ditch to be there. This decision would not damage his image, or, at least, he wouldn't add another blunder to the first.

Thus, he, too, chose the lesser of two evils: he also ran and jumped over the nonexistent ditch.

They continued their stroll as if nothing had happened. And each time they returned to the crucial spot, they went through the ridiculous ritual. But Toth's troubles were far from over.

Recent psychiatric and behavioral studies show that mountain people are more passionate and dramatic in their lovemaking than people living at lower altitudes, so they reach orgasm sooner; therefore, actual intercourse does not last as long for the mountain dweller. Consequently, on a lovely summer night like this, with business booming, Madame Giza's light went on and off at a rather rapid rate.

The two strollers, however, were not customers, so, irrespective of whether the lights were on or off, Toth and the major kept jumping in front of the busy lady's window.

To compound Toth's trouble, a local mechanic, on his way home from work, passed the two men right at the alleged ditch in front of Madame Giza's window. He greeted Major Varro with great respect. His calculated, unctuous friendliness was motivated by several factors: he was thinking of his cousin serving at the front his approaching retirement, and last, but not least, of an old charge against him: he'd allegedly committed subversion against the State. Bearing all these things in mind, he, too, jumped without a moment's hesitation. He was immediately followed by the major and his host.

Inane activities usually have unforeseen consequences. On the one hand, the outcome may be favorable: two men, two friends, might conceivably grow closer and more intimate having proved that for once in their lives they could jump like children to their heart's delight.

On the other hand, an unfavorable outcome is also possible. In this instance, unfortunately, the outcome was truly disastrous.

At first Toth felt an indefinable anxiety. The poor man blamed himself for having led his son's commander into a situation beneath his dignity. Not knowing how to make up for it, he tried to appease the major by exaggerated consideration. He ran ahead to place the major's chair under him when they got back to the porch; he bowed and scraped; he forced himself to smile.

Toth's obsequiousness did not mollify the major; indeed, his behavior reminded Varro precisely of those incidents which he would have rather forgotten. When Toth tried again to offer the major a chair, the guest ignored him and got his own. When Toth tried to turn on the charm with his most winning smile, the major gave him an icy stare in return.

Naturally these events further upset Toth, who was beset with guilt. He barely opened his mouth and when he did, he spoke almost inaudibly to emphasize his own insignificance.

This new humble image pleased the guest even less. Indeed, he considered it an open challenge. The more apologetic Toth looked, the more vigorous was the major's rejection of each attempt at reconciliation. What's more, he could not tolerate anyone he had to strain to hear; soft talk invariably drove him to distraction.

"Speak up Toth, I can't hear a word you're saying." When Toth repeated what he had said, the major would pretend he didn't understand. "I still can't hear you. Is this your idea of a joke?"

Toth felt more like crying than joking. Their friendship seemed to have come to an end; no more "my dear Toth" or "Lajos," no more extra chicken liver on his plate. He looked down and went on folding boxes petulantly, determined never to utter another sound.

Of course, he had to answer when he was asked a direct question, though he might have been better off keeping his mouth shut even then. Silence utters no words to be misinterpreted or misunderstood. There are times (minutes, hours, years, eras) when silence is the secret of longevity.

The question that caused all the subsequent trouble seemed innocent enough at first. They had been folding boxes for quite a while when the major suddenly let go of the cutting arm of the paper cutter, looked around, and asked in his usual polite tone, "Shall we retire? What time is it, Toth?"

On several previous occasions the major had not clearly understood Toth's words, but, thus far, it had always been something that could have easily been misunderstood. That this time Toth's reply did not sound even remotely like what the major thought he heard revealed the extent to which the situation had deteriorated.

Toth took out his old-fashioned pocket watch and said, "Honorable major, it's a quarter to one."

The major held his hand up to his ear. "Muttering again, eh?" he grumbled. "I can't understand a word you say."

Toth repeated what he had said, in a louder voice, articulating each word. Suddenly the major's face changed: he turned pale, his wrinkles deepened, his facial lines grew distorted, and his eyes bulged out in their sockets. The watch nearly fell out of Toth's hands. His guest, he later discovered, had heard him say, "Go screw your sweet old grandmother in the ears."

Quite understandably a military man would react violently to such an inexplicable insult. "I beg your pardon!" he yelled, banging his fist on the table. "My grandmother may have come from Skultet and been nothing more than the fifth child of the

129

local furrier, but the headmaster of the Ivanka High School felt deeply honored and privileged when on her fiftieth birthday he was permitted to bow before her and kiss her hand!"

The major turned abruptly and rushed out of the room slamming the door behind him. The Toths were stupefied. Unmistakable noises coming from their guest's room betrayed his activities: he was taking his suitcases out of the closet, opening drawers, and beginning to pack.

"He's going to leave us!" shrieked Mariska. "Now look what you've done, Lajos." Mother and daughter stared, horrified, at Toth who in turn stared ahead with glassy eyes.

Any other man confronted with such black accusatory looks would have known his duty right then: "He who insults his fellow man should make amends."

Toth, however, just sat there, the stubborn look on his face making it absolutely clear that he had no intention whatsoever of apologizing. In fact, he was rather surprised to find his wife and daughter eyeing him expectantly when it was obvious that the misunderstanding was entirely the major's fault.

"What are you two staring at me for?" he asked indignantly.

Agi vouchsafed no reply. Mariska merely sighed.

"No sighs, please!" barked Toth. "I simply said it was quarter to one. Isn't that right?"

He looked around, quite naturally waiting for the approval of his loved ones. It had always been forthcoming, even in those exceptional cases when he had been wrong; this time, however, when he was clearly right, it was not.

At first nothing happened.

Mariska remained silent and gazed at the wall with teary eyes.

Agi sadly shook her head.

Then Mariska sighed audibly and also shook her head.

Toth got angry. "What's the matter? Have you lost your tongues? Why on earth do you keep shaking your heads?"

Agi turned away as if not daring to come out with what was on her mind.

Mariska blew her nose on the right corner of her apron and

said, "We simply would like to ask you, Lajos dear, to be a little bit more careful next time."

"Mama's right!" snapped Agi, plucking up her nerve. "It's not such a good idea to speak without thinking first."

"Speak without thinking!" shouted Toth, banging his fist on the table. "I simply told the man what time it was!"

Mariska had to admit as much.

Agi admitted it too. But she did point out that people don't usually get upset over nothing. It wasn't altogether impossible that Papa had told the major the time in a way that might have been ambiguous or insulting.

Mariska agreed. If the major felt insulted, he must have had his reasons.

Toth still didn't believe that his words had sounded ambiguous, but even if they had, they most certainly had not been insulting.

Mariska said he was right: he had never insulted anyone in his life. Agi agreed, but she dimly remembered his making some reference to ears.

Mariska didn't think she'd heard the word "ears" but couldn't swear to it.

Toth claimed that it was all a figment of their imaginations. Why, for heaven's sake, would he mention anyone's ears when he was simply telling the time!

Mariska didn't argue with that.

Agi was deep in thought. The more she thought, the more she felt she'd heard her father use the word "ears" in connection with the major's grandmother.

Mariska was doing some thinking on her own and although she trusted her husband blindly, decided it would be better to say neither yes nor no to the accusation.

By now Toth had begun to lose his self-confidence. After all, it was conceivable that the word "ears" had somehow slipped out of his mouth, but he had no reason to involve the major's grandmother in any way!

Agi said she was sorry to bring it up, but she seemed to remember Papa saying weird things without any apparent reason on various occasions.

At this point Mariska began shaking her head again, though she might actually have been nodding rather than shaking.

Toth demanded to know what his daughter was hinting at.

Agi felt a bit reluctant to elaborate, but after some prodding she told how, for instance, last Wednesday in front of Klein's Beer Garden Papa had addressed Father Tomaji as "you black radish" instead of greeting him properly.

Mariska said that even though she had not been present at the time, in her opinion it was simply not possible. She would never believe her husband could utter such nonsense, although she did admit that lately the good Father had been responding rather coolly to her greetings.

Toth was aghast. Though he was unable to remember the incident, he was convinced that no salutation ever left his lips but the most reverent *Laudetur Jesus Christus*. Nevertheless the ground seemed to be sliding out from under his feet.

Then Mariska had something she wanted to get off her chest. In times like these, when Gyula's very life was at stake, she could no longer withhold the truth. From now on, she felt it was her motherly duty to remind her husband of the circumstances and events leading to his forced retirement from the railroad.

Upon hearing the word "retirement," Toth turned paprika-red.

Understandably. When one has served for nine years with irreproachable integrity, like a soldier, as a siding supervisor at the Felsopiskolc Station, and then one day, without warning or reason, is told he must retire, well, one tries to forget such a humiliating experience as quickly as possible. Mariska, on the other hand, felt that for his own sake, it was high time he faced reality and accepted the naked truth.

Toth expressed his willingness to listen—in fact, he was curious to hear what his charming wife had to say.

Mariska was more than willing to satisfy her husband's curiosity, but only on the condition that Agi cover her ears.

Agi covered her ears, and Mariska reminded him of the time when Victor Emmanuel, the king of Italy, came to the forests of northern Hungary for the autumn hunting season as the guest of the Regent, and how when the royal train passed through the flag- and flower-bedecked railroad station of Felsopiskolc, the entire staff stood at attention. At the very moment the train arrived, the siding supervisor, whose behavior up to that point had been exemplary and above reproach, broke ranks, turned his back to the slowing train, pulled down his pants, and displayed his bare behind to the stunned dignitaries looking out of the windows. . . . "Yes, that is what happened," said Mariska and burst into tears.

Lajos Toth flared up in anger.

"Not a word of it is true!" bellowed Toth. "Who told you this malicious, stupid lie?"

Mariska had been unwilling to believe that rumor until Mrs. Singer, the cashier at Mr. Berger's movie house, swore to her on a Bible that she had heard it from a most reliable source, a trustworthy eyewitness.

Toth collapsed. This was more than his integrity could endure; it took several minutes before his wife and daughter could revive him. Then they started begging him to go and apologize to the major. They each took an arm and gently, ever so gently, led him to the door. They even helped him across the threshhold.

A few hours later, at exactly 3:06 A.M. Toth ran away from home. Now obviously there was no connection between the above-mentioned episode and his departure. A mature adult does not leave home and family merely because someone misunderstands what he is trying to say. Besides, the major, with his customary magnanimity, had forgiven Toth at once, and as they went out on the porch together emphatically announced, "I beg you both not to rebuke or castigate him. We are all human beings. Isn't that so, my dear Toth?"

Toth muttered something incomprehensible. He wasn't in the best shape, but settling back into the routine of things helped him to pull himself together. There is always something comforting in work, in even the most tedious of chores. Then, too, the major was in excellent spirits—the fresh air did him good—and seemingly free of all grudges, he kept the company entertained with endless stories. Time flew by unnoticed. His audience was elated to hear that not only his general mood and appetite had considerably improved but his dreams as well. They were less depressing than the ones at the front. Last night, for instance, he'd dreamed he was a bag of itching powder emptied down the blouse of a pretty girl. He went into minute detail about how he'd penetrated deeper and deeper under the girl's clothes and how she, the dream-girl, had giggled and shrieked from his titillating touch. Everyone enjoyed the story thoroughly and laughed heartily, even Toth gave a half-smile. Who would have imagined the plans he was hatching at that very moment? Who would have thought that so soon after the resolution of the evening's first misunderstanding, another even more embarrassing one would follow?

In the midst of the general mirth, way before dawn—not too late in the new scheme of things—Lajos Toth opened his mouth and yawned! Not just a small polite yawn, but a yawn full of gusto and arrogance, right in the major's face, without any restraint, as if the guest were a doctor preparing to examine Toth's ailing tonsils.

It was bad enough that he yawned. The women vividly remembered how vehement the major's reaction had been to yawning at the beginning of his visit. Now the repeated insolence petrified them; their consternation froze their lips, halted their hands in mid-air. The two looked like a pair of birds caught in mid-flight by a hunter's bullet.

Toth had committed a grave new insult. Bad enough! At that moment he could still have saved the situation with a simple apology, but now he compounded the insult by hollering at his wife. "What are you staring at? Have I grown a horn on my forehead or something?"

When the two women described to him, in an accusatory tone, what he had done, Toth denied their charges with the obstinancy of a hardened criminal. He refused to believe his daughter; he refused to believe his loyal wife; he rejected every bit of evidence, every testimony. The argument would have dragged on indefinitely had it not been for the major, who interrupted them firmly.

"Please stop all this senseless quarreling!" he said with disarming indulgence. "What difference does it make whether we saw what we saw or Mr. Toth remembers what he remembers. If he feels that he didn't yawn, well then, he didn't mean to yawn. Only he can unravel this mystery. Think about it, dear Toth."

"I didn't have the slightest intention of yawning," shouted Toth.

"I am delighted to hear it!" replied the major. "Then am I correct in assuming that you don't feel like yawning now?"

"God forbid, not *now!*" protested Toth.

"And how about later on?" inquired the major.

"No! I wouldn't dream of it!" Toth assured him.

"Won't you perhaps forget this hasty promise later?"

"No, never!"

"Good! If you really mean it, are you willing to take the precautions necessary to prevent future yawns?"

"By all means," said Toth.

"Splendid!" replied the major. He had expected that much of a man as upright as Toth. Naturally there were several preventive methods, he said. Fortunately for the Toths, he had had some experience in this field. Night patrols at the front are often apt to yawn, a dangerous habit because a man who yawns easily falls asleep and the punishment for falling asleep at one's post in wartime is death by firing squad. But he had solved the problem: each soldier on guard duty was required to constantly suck on a plum pit and to pass it on to his replacement. "Would you happen to have a plum or a peach pit handy?"

Mariska shook her head. She was terribly sorry, but the plum season was over and the peaches weren't ripe yet. She was obviously very disturbed that this was so, but the guest consoled her.

"Never mind, dear Mariska. I'll find something else!" he said patiently, launching a feverish search through his pockets. Apparently he didn't find what he was looking for, because he jumped up and rushed to his room, where he rummaged through the chest of drawers. He came back carrying a small box camera, a container of bug powder, his service revolver, and a small framed photograph of himself (taken on the day he graduated from the military academy) leaning up against a dusty artificial palm tree, a sword dangling at his side.

"Any one of these will do," he said, studying first the objects, then Toth's mouth, "but none of them is ideal."

Suddenly he slapped his forehead. "I've got it!" he exclaimed. "The cricket!"

He took everything back to his room and returned with an egg-sized object that turned out to be a pocket flashlight. On one side was a tiny button, and when he pressed it, the flashlight both lit up and buzzed—hence the name "cricket."

He put it down in front of the fire chief. "There you are, Mr. Toth."

"What will they think of next," exclaimed Mariska in amazement. "What a clever idea!"

"And it's so simple!" applauded Agi.

Only Toth was unimpressed. Instead of being overjoyed, he examined the flashlight with open revulsion. "What am I supposed to do with it?" he asked suspiciously.

"What do you think?" laughed Agi. "Put it in your mouth, Papa, that's all there is to it."

"But be careful not to swallow it, dear," admonished Mariska.

"You shouldn't bite or swallow it," explained the major. "Just suck on it like you would a piece of candy."

But Toth was reluctant to put anything in his mouth since whatever he put in his mouth he immediately swallowed.

"There's no need to worry about that," the major assured him with a smile. "It may feel a little strange at first, but a flashlight is no harder to get used to than new dentures."

Toth remained unconvinced. His manly stature notwithstanding, he had a childish streak. Possibly he wanted more of a fuss to be made over him or perhaps he simply disliked the name "cricket." In any case he kept stalling, and as a last resort he turned to his wife and said beseechingly, "You don't want me to put this thing in my mouth, do you, Mariska?"

"Of course, Lajos. Where else?" She was genuinely astounded.

Toth looked around and then did something that befitted neither his age nor his station: he ducked under the table and hid himself. The others exchanged meaningful glances, but, as if by previous arrangement, none of them uttered a word. They just sat there waiting silently, since there was nothing better to do. They did not have long to wait. Toth climbed out from under the table. And though still sulking a bit he opened his mouth and let Mariska place the flashlight between his lips. She was as gentle as a loving mother suckling her child.

"I hope it doesn't taste too bad," she said.

Toth shook his head. The flashlight rounded out his face a bit and actually suited him rather well. Agi immediately noticed it.

"It does wonders for you, Papa!" she remarked.

When the fire chief tried to respond his tongue pressed the tiny button and the gadget buzzed and lit up behind his teeth. They all smiled.

"Let's not waste any more time!" said the major. "Can we start? I'm sure the work will go much better now."

He was right. There were no more interruptions. Toth didn't yawn once. He didn't even look tired. And if he still produced shoddy boxes, well, his co-workers were used to that by now. All these seemingly irrelevant details must be brought out to prevent anyone from trying to connect them with what followed. No one has ever run away from home just because a flashlight was placed in his mouth and for preventive purposes at that!

No wonder they were so shocked by Toth's sudden disappearance.

He was not missed right away. Presumably he had sneaked out when they stopped working and, half-dead with exhaustion, stumbled into their rooms, hardly able to keep their eyes open. Furthermore, his disappearance had gone unnoticed temporarily for another reason.

The pickup truck from the bandage works collected the finished products only once a month, and its next scheduled round was not due yet. At the Toths' house, however, as a result of the exceptional productivity of the new paper cutter

137

and the diligence of the laborers, every last bit of space was covered with boxes. Even a huge man like Toth could easily have gotten lost in that sea of boxes.

When they finally realized Toth was gone, they started calling out his name. No response. Then they searched every corner of the house, combed the garden, the neighbor's gardens, then the whole town, all the way down to the sawmill, the valley, and including the meadows on the slopes of Mt. Babony. Toth had disappeared without a trace.

Where could he be? Why did he leave? Was he in a huff over something again? Not likely. Things had been going so smoothly!

That afternoon Father Tomaji had arrived home very tired because he had had to climb the mountain twice; his duty had called him to perform last rites for the head forest ranger's mother-in-law. Upon his return, he collapsed on top of his bed just as he was in his dusty cassock. He stretched out and was just about to close his eyes when suddenly he heard someone snoring loudly.

At first the notion that he was hearing his own anticipated snores amused him. But when he held his breath for a few seconds, almost to the point of bursting, the sound persisted, unmistakably, quite audibly. With a great deal of effort (any strenuous activity was harmful because he suffered from an acute hernia), the good pastor succeeded in pulling Lajos Toth from underneath the bed. But it was much harder to arouse him and more difficult yet to make him open his mouth and speak.

Country clergymen are often misunderstood. It's a widely held misconception that most priests deliver their sermons monotonously, repeating the same phrases over and over again, and that they perform their duties like automatons. The misinformation continues: they wallow in a stupor, care only about gastronomical pleasures and so on. What no one ever mentions is that these shepherds have to deal with all sorts of devastating problems; they face such complicated imbroglios that even a cardinal might throw up his hands in despair.

For many years Matraszentanna's pastor had happily lived his life in peace and serenity. In the last few weeks, however, it seemed that his flock had suddenly gone beserk. Just the day before yesterday, for instance, a worker from the sawmill had tracked him down to complain about a strange shadow that was following him. Out in the sunshine, the worker presented the shadow—it wore the uniform of the gendarmerie. What kind of advice could Father Tomaji give the poor man? Or another case: what could the poor innocent country priest say to Prince Leonhardt, the proud owner of seventy thousand acres of woodland, when the angular old gentleman (who had English royal blood in his veins) opened his heart in the confessional booth and revealed his innermost secret—that he had become a convinced Communist. Father Tomaji could only suggest a lengthy abstinence from meat.

These minor examples demonstrate clearly how complicated his life had become and also how competently he had prepared himself to cope with the spiritual turmoil of his congregation. But Toth's confession had shaken even him. It was hard to listen without pity to the harrowing story of one of the most distinguished members of his flock. This vigorous, perfectly normal man had announced in a broken voice that his only desire in life was to hide under something.

Under what? It made no difference to Toth. And why? He couldn't tell. As his tale unravelled, it seemed that all he knew was that last night before going to bed, as he was untying his shoelaces, sitting on the edge of the bed, suddenly he was compelled to follow an internal voice which told him to go to the rectory at once. Obeying the order, Toth came over and crawled right under the pastor's bed.

The fire chief said that he had carried out these plans in full possession of his faculties. And though he admitted to being very sleepy, he was otherwise perfectly sane and fully aware of the fact that his actions would not be considered very stable. He simply could not help himself. An overpowering desire to escape had been haunting him for days. No matter where he was, in a room, in the cellar, in the open fields, he was constantly on the lookout for a safe hiding place. Even now, while chatting with the Father, he could barely resist the temptation to sneak under the clergyman's cassock.

Father Tomaji listened attentively. Standing before him was a once proud person racked with grief. The sorrows of this robust man were heavier than his body. What could he say to him?

"Well, my son," he sighed, "if it gives you a bit of relief, I don't particularly mind if you slide under my cassock for a while."

"Oh, no, thank you, Father," remonstrated Toth. "I am not about to succumb to temptation because I'm afraid it might overwhelm me altogether."

The pastor praised his will power, and then he walked up to the window and peered out at the cloudless blue sky. After deliberating for some time, he made the following moving remarks.

"What can one do for his fellowman, my dear son? We're at war and all of us are frightened. Although the actual battles are being fought in a land far away, and the newspapers daily report our victories on all fronts, we still feel a cold fear biting deeply into all of us. Why? I do not know! If I knew, I would probably stop being afraid. Think, my dear son, perhaps you could feel less troubled if you told me what's really bothering you. It's very possible that after a good talk, you will no longer feel the urge to hide yourself."

Toth bowed his head slowly and confessed that there were three things troubling him. The pastor encouraged him to go on, to reveal them all and not to leave out even the most seemingly insignificant detail.

First of all, Toth mumbled, it upset him tremendously to be forced to pull his helmet down over his eyes just because it made his guest, the honorable major, feel less anxious.

"And what else?" asked the priest.

It was the odd ritual of having to jump over the shadow of the electric transformer in front of Madame Giza's house when he went out for his evening walk with Major Varro.

"Is that so terrible?" asked the pastor, perplexed, but he hastened to extract the rest of the problem.

Toth's last complaint was the flashlight. Miserably he related how he had been forced to suck on their guest's flashlight to keep from yawning while they worked on their boxes.

The good Father asked gently whether the flashlight was very large.

Toth had to admit it was no bigger than an egg, a rather small egg at that.

The priest then wanted to know whether he had to swallow it.

No, as a matter of fact, he was not allowed to swallow it; it had to be sucked on like a piece of candy.

At this point Father Tomaji lost his patience and flew into a rage.

"Toth, this is impertinence!" he shouted. "Here we are, in the middle of a war, with people all around us trembling for their lives or weeping over their dead—and you, you have the gall to worry about such trifles, such petty piques, instead of being on your knees thanking God for guiding your son's commander to your door! You should be ashamed of yourself! Now I'm sorry that I wasted all this time on you!"

He stormed out of the room slamming the door and quickly dispatched the neighbor's young son to fetch Mariska. Then he returned to his garden and angrily paced the zigzag paths back and forth until Mariska reached his backyard, barely able to catch her breath.

"Don't look so tragic!" reprimanded the priest leading the desperate woman into the rectory. "Your crybaby husband is waiting for you in there. Please take him home."

They entered the house and looked around but Toth was nowhere to be seen. The fire chief was neither under the bed nor in the wardrobe; neither was he in the doghouse nor in the laundry hamper. Once more he had managed to vanish into thin air. This time he was not to be found until seven o'clock the next morning. As Father Tomaji was chanting the mass, his ears were suddenly assaulted by a now familiar snoring. This time the sound emanated from under the lacy altar cover. The good pastor was so startled that his mind went blank; the *Agnus Dei* got stuck in his throat and made him slightly nauseous.

The mass had to be interrupted and the parishioners thronged out puzzled and curious. The sexton was summoned and finally succeeded in dragging out Toth's huge body and pushing it into the vestry, locking the door behind him. Mariska stood there trembling, crying, gazing at the irate pastor.

"What can I do with him, Father?" Father Tomaji pensively reflected upon her question. "I have a house guest, you know. I can't stand guard over my husband all day long."

"Well, my daughter, it's rather difficult to advise you because in any decision we have to consider his feelings, too."

"Exactly! He certainly is a sensitive man! Imagine, he's not even willing to put a simple little flashlight in his mouth."

"How about tying him to his chair? At least it would keep him from running away."

"No, that won't work. My poor Lajos can't sit in one place for two minutes without falling asleep."

"Hang a bell around his neck, then," suggested the priest. "I happen to have an extra one I don't use during mass anymore."

"He'd be just like a little lamb," said Mariska smiling tenderly. Then she shook her head. "No, no it wouldn't work; the bell might irritate the major."

"Then *you* tell me what can be done with him," said the priest spreading his arms in a gesture of helplessness. "I've completely run out of ideas."

"Please have a good talk with him!" implored Mariska. "My husband has always listened to you!"

Father Tomaji rushed into the vestry and had a heart-to-heart talk with Toth. He talked about the debt a father owed his son, especially when the son was such an outstanding lad, like Gyula. This argument worked.

Toth swore on all that was holy that for the rest of the major's visit he would fight off temptation and behave like a man: he would not run away again or hide under either bed or altar.

The priest dismissed him knowing full well that when Toth made a promise, he kept it. And he was right.

Toth went straight home but refused to join the others. He

142

locked himself up in the outhouse and stayed there till dinner. After the meal he returned and again locked the door.

He was still there the next morning, but didn't answer Mariska's knock. He must have been asleep.

CHAPTER FOUR

Letter to the front:

My Dear Son,
   I hope this letter finds you in good health. When Father
Tomaji prays for our men in battle, he mentions your name first.
I want you to know that everybody is well here, but we miss you
very much. I want you to be reassured that the major is feeling
fine. At first he was rather nervous and tired but these past ten
days of rest and the fine mountain air have done wonders for
him. The first few nights he had terrible nightmares, but now he
has the funniest dreams, such as imagining he's a bag of itching
powder or that a small dog is carrying him in its mouth and tossing him up in the air. These are very fine dreams in comparison
to those he used to have, when he thought he was being ground
up and eaten and things on that order. Your father is well too,
but has become a bit absentminded and once in a while he strays
under other people's beds. Our good Father Tomaji had a long
talk with him and since then he's been all right, although sometimes he is a little withdrawn. I have other good news for you!
Major Varro has promised to take you into his barracks when
the cold weather comes. Not only that, but he said you will share
his room! I hope to God it's true! Be careful my love, take care
of yourself and your stomach! Don't eat greasy cold food. . . .
                                   Love and kisses,
                                   Mama

   She addressed the envelope and took the letter down to the
outhouse. Then very quietly, so as not to disturb their sleeping
guest, she began to talk to her husband through the closed

door. He acknowledged her presence with a discreet cough, as an indication that the place was occupied.

"How long are you planning to stay in there, Lajos?" she asked.

"What's that? Is the major leaving?" Toth inquired.

"Of course not. He won't be leaving for another four days."

"Then I'll stay in a little while longer," Toth replied.

It was Sunday. The bells were ringing and Mariska did not want to be late for church, so she slid the letter and a pencil through a crack in the door. Toth signed the letter.

Mariska put on her Sunday outfit. "I'm going to church," she told Agi who was plucking a chicken on the porch. "Your father is sitting in the outhouse; the major is asleep. Look after them, my love!"

She kissed her daughter and left.

About fifteen minutes later, a towsled major in pajamas stepped out of his room, sleepily greeted Agi with a yawn, and muttered "Good morning." Then he headed for the outhouse.

Agi gazed after him with concern.

Before the major arrived, the Toth marriage had been exemplary: Mariska adored her husband, thought him superior to everyone, and obeyed blindly when he as much as blinked his eyes. Agi worshipped her father, as teenage girls often do. Everything beautiful in the world was epitomized by her Papa: the melting of chocolate in her mouth, the whirring of sparrows, the smell of a red rose, the thrill of being alive—all this and more. The absolute totality of beauty and perfection culminated in her father.

Soon after the major's arrival, however, the two women underwent a profound change: their old loyalties were replaced by new ones. In Mariska's soul the change had crept in gradually; in Agi it took place with lightning speed. Physical attraction tends to be the most fickle of all reactions. Although she had always loved the coloring and smell of her father's skin, now she was only attracted by the major's. Instead of her father's voice, it was the reverberation of the major's alto that

145

thrilled her. Even the major's boots had replaced her father's in her affections. She worked long and hard to retain the luster on the guest's footwear. Later she even took them to bed, played with them, and sang to them as if they were precious dolls.

Adult women, in general, and our charming Mariska in particular, are reluctant to discard deep emotions so casually. Therefore, although she sided with her husband during those senseless arguments, she secretly felt her guest wanted only what was best for her husband. Nevertheless, she still wouldn't resort to open disavowal of her man even though she too had come under the major's spell. With her the attraction was not so much physical as spiritual, perhaps even transcendental. Her whole being seemed consumed by a powerful desire to make the major's stay as pleasurable as possible. Her concern for his welfare had grown into a fixation. She sensed when he was thirsty and immediately brought him a *spritzer*. She even anticipated his farts and would unobtrusively leave the room so as to avoid embarrassing him. In sum she had become a protective shield, a living barricade whose sole function and divine duty it was to guard her guest against any vexation or unnecessary disturbance.

Mariska's sensitivity grew day by day. This was partially due to her lack of adequate sleep and the resulting tension, also her ceaseless worry—first for her son, and later for her husband as well. As time passed she became a telepathic phenomenon: she was capable of sensing the mildest ripple in the major, even from a considerable distance. She would hear noises, see signs, and have visions that forewarned her of any impending danger threatening the beloved guest.

For instance, in one corner of the porch there was an old umbrella standing against the wall—it had been left behind by one of their visitors. For no apparent reason this umbrella sometimes fell over onto the floor.

One morning, the major was dozing and Mariska was standing in line in front of the butcher shop (meat was rationed in those days). It was almost her turn when a man on a bicycle stopped and asked, "Is there anybody here named Mrs. Toth?"

For months people tried to convince her that this incident was nothing but an hallucination, a trick that her overtaxed nerves played upon her. But she was adamant and assured everyone that the person on the bicycle was an old, gentle, Jewish man with a gray beard—the unmistakable image of St. Peter.

"Yes, I'm Mrs. Toth," she replied. "What is it?"

"You better watch out for that umbrella!" he warned. And with that the heavenly messenger was gone.

Fortunately the butchershop was not too far from home for—miracle of miracles—just as Mariska reached the porch she caught the umbrella in mid-air, thereby preventing it from falling over, and most likely awakening the major.

On that fine Sunday morning, at the end of the mass, Mariska heard another divine message. This time no one appeared, but in the middle of the soothing harmony of the organ she seemed to hear a peculiar, discordant sound, like a scratchy voice coming from a loudspeaker, saying, "Attention please! Mrs. Lajos Toth, *née* Mariska Balogh, is wanted urgently in front of the outhouse."

The other parishioners either could not hear this message or failed to grasp its special significance. Be that as it may, Mariska sprang up at once, forged her way through the thick crowd, and rushed home prepared for the worst.

As she entered her yard, she saw a group of people clustered around the outhouse, shouting, and hammering on the door. What on earth could they want? And why was Agi sobbing on the porch, like a forlorn bird? And why was the major tossing his clothes into his suitcase? Goodness gracious!

"I've had enough of this!" Mariska heard her guest shouting. The poor man's face was contorted with pain and his voice trembled as he cried: "Come and help me! I don't want to miss the bus!"

The bees were buzzing and the hollyhocks were in full bloom. Major Varro stopped in front of the outhouse door. It was closed. He walked around in the garden for a while, but still the door did not open. Returning, the major knocked gently. Toth coughed once meaningfully.

The major went back to his room. By now Agi was at work on the second chicken. Later the major reappeared and purposefully rushed to the outhouse. He knocked on the door. An admonishing cough was the only response. Once more the major walked, waddled, tottered back to the house.

Agi noticed the major's disappointment and felt obliged to say something.

"Isn't it a lovely day, sir?"

The major muttered something inaudible.

"The sun is shining but it's really not that hot."

Not even a mutter. Seemingly disgruntled, he dashed into his room.

When he returned from the garden for the third time, without success, his face was yellow, his eyes red, and his pupils had widened. Agi smiled at him broadly.

"May I ask you something, Honorable Major, please?"

He stopped and stared at her.

"I was wondering, sir, whether you have ever felt extremely happy for no reason at all? And then, for no reason, have you suddenly felt depressed? I mean . . . have you ever felt like giggling one minute and crying the next?"

Her hero gave no response, instead, he was gone. His feet pounded in the hall and seconds later the shattering slam of his bedroom door reverberated through the house.

Now Agi felt both concerned and responsible. It was time to act. Hastily she changed her white, high-necked cotton blouse for a low-cut light blue embroidered top. She turned up its collar in such a way as to emphasize the loveliness of her budding beauty. Then she unbraided her hair and let it fall loose and long. When the major returned to the porch for the fourth time, Agi was waiting for him in a provocative pose.

"Major, sir, this time I would like to ask you a favor," she said, stepping up to him and flashing a flirtatious smile.

The rugged soldier tried to stand erect, clenched his teeth, and attempted to return the smile.

"I would like to ask you, Major, to look at me and say the very first thing that comes to your mind."

She closed her eyes. Her heart was pounding rapidly. She stood there trembling expectantly, breathing heavily through parted lips.

At first all she could hear were the major's teeth grinding. This sounded rather carnivorous, almost bloodthirsty, but a girl in love might very easily construe it in an entirely different way. Finally he spoke, his voice barely disguising his fury.

"Who the hell is in the outhouse?"

Agi's eyes widened with fear.

"If your beloved papa wants to play tricks or spite me," he shouted in a menacing tone, "he'll soon learn who I am."

Stoutly he marched back into his room, jerkily pulled down his suitcase, and amidst grunting and cursing, began to pack frantically. Agi lost her head; in a heedless panic she raced out into the street crying for help.

Since the street was crowded with Sunday strollers, it was no surprise that within minutes a horde of passers-by had clustered by the Toths' gate. But nobody knew what the trouble was and listening to Agi's incoherent babbling didn't help. Who was sitting in the outhouse and why? Who was going to leave and why? The consensus was that enemy parachuters had landed in the back yard and were hiding among the hollyhocks and occupying the outhouse. The townspeople began to hurl rocks and shout insults and curses at the imaginary intruders. Those who knew some English swore in English.

This was the state of affairs when Mariska arrived gasping for breath. Squealing hysterically, she dismissed the uninvited busybodies, ran down to the outhouse, and began pounding her fist on the door. Only a polite cough came as a response.

Utterly shaken, the desperate woman rushed back to the house, directly to the major's room. She implored him to be a little bit more patient. Without waiting for an answer, she ran out of the house and crossed over to Professor Cipriani's mansion.

The world-renowned psychiatrist had always been extremely fond of the Toths: Mariska was the only one allowed to wash his shirts; Toth was the privileged one who broke in all his shoes and hats—only after Toth had worn the new items for a week would the Professor find them comfortable enough for his own wear. Even suits seemed to fit him better after Toth had tried the garments on.

On this serene Sunday morning, the revered man had been relaxing; still he jumped up quickly to meet the visibly shaken Mariska and willingly accompanied her to the outhouse and banged on the door himself.

"It's Dr. Cipriani, Mr. Toth. I've come to talk to you for a while."

All resistance stopped. The door swung open at once and Toth sullenly yielded his much coveted position to the major. He meekly followed the professor to his study. There the conscientious doctor thoroughly examined him and, upon finishing, patted Toth's shoulder with visible satisfaction.

"Congratulations, my friend, you are in excellent health. Now tell me, what's bothering you?"

The doctor peered at the patient with a confidence-inspiring kindness: his broad forehead, gray goatee, and soothing voice finally peeled off the protective shield and Toth opened his heart to him.

"Nothing really, doctor. It's just that I can't understand what people want from me. I've done everything I could: I pulled my helmet down over my eyes making myself look like a drunken truck driver; I stopped yawning and stretching; I gave up crawling under Father Tomaji's bed—and *that* hasn't exactly been easy! And realizing that our son's life depended on it, I even trained myself not to spit out the flashlight they put in my mouth. Now I ask you, what more can be expected of a father? And why is it such a great crime to sit leisurely in the outhouse?"

"How fascinating," said the world-renowned psychiatrist, his interest piqued. "Tell me, do you find that putting the flashlight in your mouth gives you diarrhea?"

"Oh, no! My digestion is perfectly normal. I sit in the outhouse simply because I like to. It's nice there. Nobody bothers me, and after locking the door I find a cozy position, almost as lovely as sitting in my beloved mother's lap. So, why on earth do they pound on the door? Is this a crime? Am I abnormal? Do I have a disease?"

"It's not a disease at all!" smiled Cipriani. "It's only a symptom, dear Toth. . . . Have you enjoyed sitting in the outhouse for a long time now?"

"Oh, no," said Toth. "It's a very recent habit. In fact, come to think of it, it's only been since the major arrived that I've preferred this place to the porch."

"Aha, that's what I suspected!" nodded the professor. "May I ask you to stand up for a minute, please?"

Toth obeyed. Cipriani looked him up and down.

"How tall are you, dear Toth?"

"I guess I'm a bit taller than average."

"And what about your distinguished guest? Is he shorter than you?"

"He comes up to my shoulder at the most."

"Well, there's the rub my dear friend," concluded the world-renowned psychiatrist. "You are both victims of a difference in height. You can't expect a major to look up to you all day long, can you? Admit it. Put yourself in his shoes."

"I get it," said Toth, "but I don't see how I can change my size."

The professor smiled again. "Nowadays there are cures for far more complicated problems: when the plague is virtually eliminated, rabies can be remedied, and puerperal fever is nothing more than a nightmarish memory, complaints such as yours don't present any problem—they are mere child's play. The simplest solution would be to have the major stand on a little stool. But then again he might fall off and hurt himself, which would destroy his whole vacation and perhaps lead to unforeseen consequences. I suggest that you, dear Toth, put up with some temporary discomfort."

"I would gladly give up breathing," declared Toth, "but even that won't make me shorter than the major."

"Actually, all you have to do," replied the professor, "is simply bend your knees a bit."

Toth gasped.

"You mean I should bend my own knees?" he repeated, dumbfounded.

"You won't feel a thing, my dear man."

"Temporarily or permanently?"

Dr. Cipriani did not think it would be healthy to constantly change positions so he suggested that Toth pull up his knees even in bed. Gradually this position would become second nature to him.

Toth sank into deep thought.

"No," he said a short while later. "I can't do it!"

"Forget your vanity!" the doctor said with a frown. "Think of your son. Honestly, what's worse—bending your knees a bit or making Gyula's commander angry?"

That was the decisive argument. Although still reluctant, Toth was unable to refute it, and heaving a mournful sigh, he slowly bent his knees. At once he seemed at least a head shorter.

"Is that enough?" he asked.

"Yes," consented the learned doctor. "Not even the world's shortest major could ask for anything more."

"If you think it will help, I can bend a little more."

"Don't overexert yourself. That's fine. Now, let's see how well you can walk."

Toth managed admirably. Could he run? Yes, he could. And sit down, stand up, climb the bookshelf ladder, pick flowers. His performance was remarkable. With the exception of his bent knees, Toth's movements looked perfectly natural.

"Now you can go home in peace," said the professor. "And think of the reception you'll get!"

But the thought of going home depressed Toth terribly. From the window where he was standing, he could get a full view of the main street of Matraszentanna. It was crowded with happy people parading in their Sunday suits. He knew every one of them. They all knew him, too. No matter how you looked at it, there wasn't a soul out there walking with bent knees.

"You don't expect me to walk down the street like this, do you, Doctor? People will point their fingers at me!"

"Come on, don't be conceited, my friend!" Cipriani shook his head. "Do you think you're the only one? You're wrong Toth, dead wrong! Listen friend, in today's world we all have to make sacrifices!"

The world-renowned psychiatrist went on consoling his friend by telling him how extremely common such complaints had been in his practice. Every era has its own fashionable illness: in ours no one is satisfied with his own build. Most people would like to look a head shorter, but there are midgets who view themselves as giants. Medical science is powerless because there is no such thing as absolute measure. The only thing that counts is how tall or heavy each individual considers himself to be. The *Acta Medica Hungarica* had recently carried an article by a Jewish doctor, who claimed that even though his waist is one hundred and ten centimeters, he regularly left his apartment through the keyhole and returned home in the same fashion. If medical ethics didn't bind him, Professor Cipriani would cite many more examples from his own practice. But, in the circumstances, he could only assure the fire chief that a bent knee was the least a father could do for his son.

"Let's have a trial run," he suggested. "Why don't you walk a short distance with bent knees and watch how people react. If it makes you feel better, I'll go with you."

Toth accepted his generous offer gratefully. They started out on the street at a busy corner, full of people. And what happened? Nothing happened. Children waved at him from a distance; adults nodded respectfully; some even stopped to ask about his family and his distinguished guest. Everything went on as usual. Then he heard a strange, animal-like giggling.

It came from none other than Uncle Gyuri, the demented mailman, who had worshipped Toth as if he were a god. Out of nowhere he suddenly stepped before his idol and went down on all fours, circling around him and barking like a dog.

The professor waved him aside.

"What can you expect?" he said to Toth with a knowing smile. "He's been in my clinic three times already but there is nothing anyone can do for him." A few minutes later he bid farewell to Toth, who clearly no longer needed his support. The passers-by noticed nothing peculiar about Toth: in fact, they treated him with more respect than ever. For instance, Prince Leonhardt of Luxembourg, who was out walking his Russian wolfhounds, stopped, grinned, and shaking his finger conspiratorially addressed Toth in broken Hungarian: "Valking? Valking? Sure valking after girls, no?" What a remarkable scene! The prince had barely acknowledged Toth's greetings in the past.

If these incidents were not sufficient for Toth, the reception he received at home certainly should have put him at complete ease. Mariska welcomed him cheerfully as always, and not even Agi spotted anything—Agi who used to notice the smallest speck of dust on his uniform. The major, who had just come out of his room, freshly shaven and redolent of cologne, cast a piercing glance at him.

Suddenly the major returned to his room, then came out again. This time he examined Toth more carefully, recognizing that something was slightly different.

After a third curious scrutiny, he finally asked, "Tell me, Toth, what have you done to yourself?"

"Nothing," said Toth.

"I, I don't know . . . ," the puzzled major said measuring him with his eye. "You look a whole head taller somehow!"

Now Toth was quite sure he was a head shorter, but what counted was that his guest seemed satisfied with the change. Professor Cipriani's predictions had proved correct. Not now, not later, did anyone ever notice that he was bending his knees.

Most people would have been happy or at least satisfied. One couldn't desire any more or any less than the present equilibrium. When they sat down to dinner, the major almost smothered Toth with kindness and openly displayed his friendly attitude. Toth, however, sat stiffly with an immobile,

154

dour face, hardly touching his food, and the minute they let their guard down, he slipped away.

"Lajos! Oh, Lajos, where are you, my sweet?" shouted Mariska out the porch door.

The only answer was a discreet cough coming from the direction of the blooming hollyhocks.

For a while they left him in peace. But when he had failed to emerge by mid-afternoon, Mariska decided to take matters into her own hands. First she implored him to come out, then she tried cunning, logic, and last she appealed to his decency. Nothing worked. The miserable woman finally lost her patience.

"Listen, Lajos, I'm going to count up to three," she said in a tone unusually harsh, "and if you don't come out I'll go fetch the locksmith."

Like talking to a stone wall! Toth sullenly kept silent and locked up.

What was to be done? Frustrated, she went back to the major and gave an elaborate explanation of her husband's disappearance, desperately beating about the bush in her attempts to cover up Toth's stubbornness.

"Funny, I was under the impression that Mr. Toth was suffering from some kind of intestinal irregularity," remarked the major. "Are you saying that he's holed up in that place because he enjoys it?"

Mariska had to admit this without any additional whitewashing. But her fear that the major would fall into another rage or show some sign of displeasure proved unfounded.

On the contrary—the major looked exceptionally cheerful and relaxed. Casually he turned to Agi and asked whether she had the time and inclination to bring him two large bottles of ice-cold beer from Klein's. Then equipping himself with an opener and two glasses, he walked over to the outhouse. Placing the bottles on the ground, he knocked politely.

"Don't think for a minute, my dear Toth, that I want to oust you from your place. I've just come down for a short visit.

155

I brought you a bottle of ice-cold beer. You like light beer, I presume?"

"I like any kind of beer," replied Toth from within, "and if you don't look down your nose at my humble throne, I'll gladly share it with you. Come in and take a seat."

Unlatching the door, he apologized for the lack of space and moved over into a corner. Though it was a rather tight squeeze, they both managed to fit. There was room for the beer bottles on the floor but they had to hold their glasses.

For the first few minutes Toth felt somewhat ill at ease, which was only natural: he had never been at such close quarters with so high ranking a dignitary.

Later the fire chief apologized for the primitive facility. In a small village like this, he claimed, one could not expect much more.

The major reassured him that this tiny abode was quite satisfactory and suited his needs adequately.

Toth now regretted not having had it cleaned. Though he had ordered the pump, the peculiar sanitation man talked him out of it; it was he who had objected to a thorough cleaning prior to the major's arrival.

"Why bother with cleaning?" asked the major. "Am I such a demanding guest?"

"No, the honorable major is not at all demanding, but there have been other guests in the past who complained about the smell."

The major shook his head—Toth had always misunderstood him. If he remembered correctly, he hadn't once complained about anything, least of all about the outhouse, which was more than adequate.

"Well," continued Toth with his customary modesty, "we may not have much to offer, but we do try our best!"

"Frankly, if I were you, I'd never leave this place!" remarked the major.

"I don't really want to unless it's absolutely necessary," Toth hastened to add.

"Smart man! To your health. Listen. Can you hear the leaves rustling?"

"To yours, honorable Major! Yes, I can."

"And what's buzzing here?"

"Some kind of bug."

"What is it called?"

"The green gadfly."

"What a pretty name!" the major nodded with approval.

For a while they sat there in tranquility listening to the buzzing of gadflies and the whispering of the leaves. But it's an age-old axiom that all good things must come to an end.

"Unfortunately it's time for me to go," said the major standing up. "Enjoy yourself, dear Toth."

"Thank you for the visit, Major!"

"Let's face it, Toth, we did have minor disagreements to start with, but now I hope everything is all settled."

"Praise to the Lord!" said Toth standing up as well. "Do come again any time you want."

"Certainly, as soon as I can. Will we have the pleasure of your company box making tonight?" he asked gently.

"Why, of course," Toth assured his guest.

"Until then, have a good time," said the major. "But before I go, I would just like to say how happy it makes me to know that in these trying times, when so many people feel lost, there is at least one man who has found his place in life." The major sauntered away.

The last days of Major Varro's leave were uneventful and monotonous. Everyone was content: whenever they could, the Toths slept; when they had to make boxes, they made boxes. Equilibrium had been restored.

One curious change, however, should be recorded for the sake of the truthful presentation of events: Lajos Toth suddenly became genuinely interested in box making. What he had thus far considered as forced labor had now become his prime hobby; indeed, he worked so hard that soon his boxes were of the highest quality. The others passed them around, admiring his exquisite workmanship.

"Hurray for Papa!" Agi exclaimed.

"Who would have believed it?" said the major, shaking his head in amazement.

"You see, Lajos my sweet," sighed Mariska, "with a little bit of good will one can perform miracles!"

But the Toths paid dearly for their peace and quiet. They were exhausted beyond endurance now. Lack of sleep, constant anxiety, the stress and strain of it all had taken their toll. Mariska started dropping things although she was extra careful. Sometimes, with her eyes wide open, she fell asleep standing up, like a hen hypnotized for an experiment.

Instead of dropping things, Agi bumped into them. Once, in a dark room, she fell over her father several times, and turning on the lights didn't seem to help: she collided with him each time she got up. "Excuse me," she said, backing into the ironing board and rebounding toward her father. Toth could have stepped aside, there was enough space, yet he, too, lurched forward in the direction of his daughter. The result had all the impact of two locomotives colliding head on. Both of them were so tired they had reached their saturation point, a level of fatigue at which darkness no longer seemed any different from light.

The real gravity of Toth's condition, however, lay beneath the surface. During the last four days of the major's visit he went around in a fog. His head was constantly buzzing. This condition did not disturb him, rather it made him feel senile. It was a peculiar weakness, a slow fading. To begin with, he had become hard of hearing, and people had to raise their voices when they talked to him. Once in a while he would forget to swallow his food; pieces of meat could remain in his mouth from noon till night. He would confuse the most routine activities, trying for example, to comb his hair with a bottle of soda water. At the farewell dinner, while eating his chicken soup, he got the mistaken notion that it was already time for coffee and a cigar. He customarily blew the smoke through his nose, but his startled companions suddenly noticed that the chicken soup, vegetables, even Mariska's delectable little dumplings were gushing down from his nostrils.

But no one paid heed to these minor irregularities. Only one thing was important: that their guest was content, happy, and at ease. Their success was confirmed not only by the fact that in the last two weeks he had put on about four kilos, but also by a sentiment he expressed as they stood waiting for his bus at the station.

"Believe me, dear friends, I don't have the slightest desire to leave."

Mariska sighed deeply, a manifestation of her joy. "We are also saddened by your departure, honorable Major!" she added, genuinely moved.

"With you, dear Toth," the major turned to Lajos, "I am thoroughly delighted—you have made great strides. But you must be careful not to fall back into your former ways."

Toth stared at him blankly and muttered something between his teeth. The words were audible only to Mariska who was standing right by him; what she thought she heard was, "Oh, go pee in your pants!"

It will remain a mystery forever whether she was right or not because at that very moment the bus pulled in with an ear-splitting roar that overpowered every other sound. When the bus came to a complete halt, the major shook hands with each of the Toths in turn and even gave Agi a quick peck on the forehead.

"God be with you all! Under your hospitable roof I have embarked on a new life. I am not a man of many words. I'd rather express my appreciation by deeds and show my gratitude with action."

The Toths were moved to tears. The major boarded the bus, then leaned out a window and said, "Once more, thanks for your kind hospitality!"

"We are so glad you enjoyed your stay, Major, sir."

"All the best, dear Toths!"

"Have a good trip, honorable Major."

The bus started. The major yelled in passing, "I hope I wasn't a nuisance to you!"

"Oh no! Not at all!" they shouted back, smiling and waving.

When the bus finally disappeared around a corner, the Toths were still waving but their farewell smiles vanished one, two, three, like candles blown out in succession.

Toth didn't move. Still holding his arm in waving position, he was peering at the curve as if he were afraid the bus would turn around and deliver the major back, starting everything all over again. When this didn't happen he gradually began to relax. The first thing he did was take off his helmet and put it back on properly, so that its vertical edge made a ninety degree angle with his body's horizontal axis. Next he tried to straighten out his knees.

"Help, my dear Mariska," he groaned, because his knees had become rigid in their new position. At last, with the aid of both women, he straightened his knees. Then he stretched himself out, and, flanked by his family, his head held high, he set off for home filled with pride and confidence. Once there, he marched straight to the paper cutter without a glance to either left or right. The monstrous contraption barely made it through the doorway, and Toth had a terrible time lugging the thing all the way to the hollyhocks behind the outhouse. Back on the porch after his panting subsided, he announced, "From today on we shall eat breakfast in the morning, dinner in the evening, and go to bed at night. Is that clear?"

"Everything will be just the way you want it, my dear Lajos," said Mariska with a disarming smile of consent.

And so it was. When evening came on they ate supper, and when they finished Toth pulled the big armchair near the swinging door and sank into it. Mariska snuggled up to him and pulled Agi into her father's lap; she clung to him like a twining vine around an old oak tree. Above them the August sky glimmered, scattering its stardust generously. Mt. Babony, like a giant green lung, exhaled its fresh evening breeze onto them. Winter was just around the corner. . . . And how inhuman those Russian winters were: those bone-chilling gales, the harsh freezing cold. . . . But the major's quarters would certainly be well-heated. Military leaders live in stone or brick houses and have double guards to protect them at night. Those privileged few should certainly be out of danger.

160

Inventory:

Taken by Karoly Kincs of the Gomel Military Hospital. Witnessed by Sergeant L. Koroda and D. Boglar. The following items have been found among the belongings of Ensign Gyula Toth. P.S. Items originally belonging to the Army are not listed herewith.

Item: One undershirt   Description: Silk
Item: One handkerchief   Description: Checkered
Item: One wallet with   Description: 10.60 (in assorted
    money   bills and coins)
Item: One pencil   Description: Indelible
Item: One photo   Description: One male, one female
Item: One pack of cigarettes Description: —
                     Date, signature

                    (Disintegrated in the rain barrel.)

Mariska smiled at her husband.

"You must be very tired. Let's go to bed, Lajos, dear."

"All right, but first I'll have a cigar," announced Toth.

Mariska jumped for the cigar box, Agi reached for a match. Toth inhaled his much missed aromatic smoke with sensual pleasure. He did love the small joys of life. He was in such a good mood that, stretching until his joints cracked, he sighed, "Oh Mother, Mother, dear old Mother!"

At that very moment they heard familiar steps approaching. The Toths looked up in utter disbelief.

Suitcase in hand, Major Varro appeared in the doorway. He was beaming.

"I can see, dear friends, that you can't believe your eyes. But it's me all right!"

The general consternation still prevailed. Suddenly Toth emitted an odd popping sound. It was not a human sound. It was the sound a bubble makes, the last bubble a drowning man sends to the surface.

"I was going to get my pass stamped at the headquarters in Eger, but the station's commander told me the good news: the partisans have blown up a bridge so there will be no transport back to the front for at least three days. . . ."

He smiled at Toth, then at Mariska, and finally at Agi.

"Since it was so hard for me to part with you, I thought I'd come back to my dear friends, the Toths, and spend these extra days with you. . . . I trust it won't be inconvenient? . . ."

They were still mute. Energetically the major carried his suitcase to his room and returned with a suggestion: "If you don't have anything better to do," he said bursting with energy, "we might just make a few more boxes."

He fell silent and looked around.

"Goodness!" he exclaimed. "What's happened to the paper cutter, dear Toth? Where is it?"

Toth made several attempts to reply, but only after the third try did he manage to get out the words in an unnatural voice, high-pitched and scratchy, "What? Paper cutter? It's out there in the garden, honorable Major, sir."

"In the garden? But why?" cried the major, bewildered. "And where?"

"Down there by the hollyhocks," answered Toth dutifully. "I'd be glad to show it to you."

They disappeared into the darkness.

Mariska and Agi stayed behind staring into the dark. They could see nothing. For a while nothing happened. Then a dull thud was heard. They shuddered. Then another thud with a grating, grinding sound—the cutting arm of the huge paper cutter had slammed down again. They shuddered even more. Finally—one last whack of the blade. . . .

Some time elapsed before Toth came back to the house.

"What are you standing there for?" he asked. "Let's go to bed."

They quickly got ready for bed and climbed in. They had been lying there a while when Mariska inquired diffidently, "Did you cut him in three, Lajos dear?"

"Three? No. I cut him into four equal parts. Why? Wasn't that right?"

"Of course it was right, my dearest!" said Mariska. "You always know what's best."

They lay there in silence, shifting position from time to time.

Since their bodies were so inhumanly tired, they soon fell asleep. Toth, however, continued tossing and turning rather violently. He kept groaning and moaning in his dreams. Once he almost fell off the bed.

A nightmare perhaps? That would be strange indeed—such a thing had never happened to him before.